The Moving Pictures

An Ella Graepenteck
Genealogy Mystery

Erika Maren Steiger

E. STEIGER & CO.
LOS ANGELES

Published 2021 by E. Steiger & Co.
www.esteigerandco.com

Cover design by James, GoOnWrite.com

in fervent gratitude to Raymond Chandler and Los Angeles, both underappreciated by the world at large and both deeply loved by me

Table of Contents

Chapter 1: Summer in Los Angeles

My rear view mirror told me the driver behind me was in a terrible mood, and those to my left and right didn't look much happier, but I thought the day had potential. There were enough clouds to keep the sun from landing hard on cars and bouncing into my eyes. The Santa Ana winds had tired themselves out, and the voice on the radio said the latest brush fire was 98% contained. Traffic was moving on the 10, not quickly, but moving, and I had pushed my deep distrust of coincidences so far back in my mind that I had not the slightest sense of impending danger. In fact, I thought it was shaping up to be a better than average Monday.

The radio cut out because my phone rang. The number showing on the dashboard looked familiar, but I couldn't place it. I decided to answer it anyway, and pressed the little button on the steering wheel. I had to say hello twice before I got a response.

"Ms. Graepenteck? This is Bob Ogilvie." He pronounced it GRAPP-in-teck. Almost right, and an understandable mistake, since all our previous communication had been by email.

"Yes, this is Ella Graepenteck."

"Oh, sorry. GRAPE-in-teck."

"No problem. How are you, Mr. Ogilvie?"

"Oh, please, call me Bob. I just want to let you know I'm running a little late. I apologize. Harvey, my partner, should be there, so you can go ahead and have a seat. I won't be long. I'm sorry for any inconvenience."

"It's okay, Bob. Thanks for letting me know."

Bob and his partner were dealers in old Hollywood memorabilia. They were particular specialists in the 1920s. I happen to be related to a minor twenties moviestar called Reginald Ellis, real name Lester Hodelman Jr. He was my first cousin, twice removed. His mother and my great grandmother were sisters. I had never gotten around to exploring his movie career in any depth, but I did once find him in a library collection of 1920s gossip magazines, almost always accompanied by his best friend, another actor called Edmund Walforth, who seemed to generate unsavory rumors wherever he went. Reginald was drunk in public from time to time, but Edmund was seen with gangsters and rabble rousers and many, many different women. He must have been a chronic headache for the studio scandal squashers.

I was meeting Bob for Sara Markis, a new client I had met for the first time the previous Thursday. I had gone that day to her apartment at 1873 Bluebird Avenue, just south of Santa Monica Boulevard in Westwood. A realtor might call the building Parisian style, but it had looked to me like something a few real estate developers dreamed up late at night, in a bar, in 1985. It was four stories, plus an underground entry and garage, and each floor had a different style of ironwork balcony rail. The walls of the top floor were covered in curved terra cotta roof tiles, and the lower floors were stucco the color of wet sand. If you tried hard and had had a few drinks you might be able to imagine the top floor apartments as romantic little artists' garrets, but inside they were probably generic one or two bedroom condominiums. They would sell for at least $600,000 each, maybe closer to $800,000. I didn't hold her choice of building against my client. Not much, anyway. Plenty of people would spend more on worse.

Sara's apartment was on the third floor, just below the fake attic. She was a tiny blonde who had not lost any of her youthful energy, despite having reached the age of at least twenty-two. She had her phone in her hand as she answered the door, and she typed away at it with both thumbs while she tilted her head slightly to the right, flashed bright blue eyes briefly at me, smiling, and said, "Hi! Come in! Thanks for coming!"

I followed her into the living/dining area, closing the door behind me, and sat where she indicated, next to her on a wide white sofa with a high, curved back. The whole place was white, the floors, the walls, the countertops, and the upholstery, in shades from snow to ecru. The fabric on the sofa was smooth, with a raised jacquard pattern. It was pretty, on its own, but in that environment it was just debris flying past in a tornado of white.

There was a document on the glass topped coffee table. I pointed at it.

"Is this a copy of the birth certificate?"

She took a moment to finish what she was typing and then put her phone down on the table.

"Yes! You can go ahead and look at it. You can even have that one. I have another copy, and my grandmother

4

has more. Her birth name was Lily, which is such a pretty name, but her real name, I mean, the name she grew up with, the name her parents, her adoptive parents gave her is Emily, which is also a nice name, but it's weird to think she might have been Lily, you know? But anyway, yeah, you can see it there."

I picked it up. Sure enough, it was a birth certificate that indicated that Lily Frances Walsh was born in 1926 to Ellen Marie Walsh and Edmund Walforth. Lily had her mother's last name rather than her father's, because her parents were not married, but the fact that his name appeared on the certificate indicated he officially acknowledged parentage, and was most likely present at the hospital at the time of birth. This document warranted careful study. I was able to examine it in silence for a full two seconds before Sara started speaking again.

"Yeah, so, like I said, we already know all about her birth mother, about Ellen, but no one has been able to find out anything about her birth father, just nothing at all, and it would be so great to have that, because she's going to be ninety this year, my grandmother, and it would just be such a great gift to give, to be able to tell her about her father, you know, who he was, something about his family, where he came from, that sort of thing."

"Yes, well, I hope I can find that information for you. If this Edmund Walforth is the same one I know a little about, then I can understand why it has been hard to track him down."

"You said he was a moviestar? How amazing is that! I mean, wow!"

"A minor moviestar. He was never very famous, so he probably didn't show up in regular newspapers, just industry publications. Also, Edmund Walforth probably wasn't his real name, so he most likely wouldn't be under that name in census records or other ordinary documentation."

"But that name is on the birth certificate."

"Yes, and that may mean it is not the same person, or that he legally changed his name. There could be a number of explanations."

"But you can find out, right? I mean, what the explanation is?"

"I can do my best. No genealogist can guarantee results. I will try every way I can think of, but you do need to understand that you will be paying me for my time and expertise, not for the answers to your questions. It's possible the documentation you're seeking doesn't exist."

She stared at me for a moment, her face blank and her head still. I had never seen eyes that were such a bright blue, at least not in person. I wondered if she might be related to Paul Newman. She blinked and went back to her previous animated state.

"Well, you're the first one who knew anything about this moviestar guy, which seems like a pretty good sign to me, so I say let's do it!"

I had already done some preliminary online searching and found no one named Edmund Walforth in the Los Angeles area in the 1920s, which supported the hypothesis that it wasn't his real name, but if that were true, why was it on the birth certificate? It was an intriguing question that seemed likely to lead to more intriguing questions. Experience has made me suspicious of coincidences, and the fact that I happened to have a personal, if distant, connection to the exact person Sara was looking for certainly was one, but the possibilities were compelling. I couldn't resist. I was hired.

The next day, Friday, I had discovered Bob Ogilvie and sent him an email. He claimed to have a large number of documents belonging to California Pictures, the long defunct studio that had employed both Edmund Walforth and Reginald Ellis. I was hoping there might be something there that would give Edmund's real name, or at least a clue to where he came from. I wrote Bob that I had a client who believed she was related to Edmund Walforth, and if I could prove the connection, said client might be interested in purchasing things related to him, although I couldn't guarantee it. That was good enough for Bob, and we set a meeting for 10:30 on Monday. That was where I was driving that morning, thinking it was looking like a pretty good day. I probably had a smile on my face.

Chapter 2: Bob Ogilvie's Office

I worked my way rightward across the lanes and made it to my exit, feeling a small but genuine sense of accomplishment for having done so. Traffic on La Brea was worse than it had been on the 10, but since I already knew Bob would be late, I wasn't concerned. I passed by auto repair shops and laundromats, motels with broken signs and worn out apartment buildings with bars on the windows. After a familiar series of curves in the road I passed the sign saying I was in the Miracle Mile District, an artifact, like the magazines that mentioned Reginald Ellis and Edmund Walforth, of the 1920s, and one of the areas most responsible for L.A.'s being such a car-centric town. Its creation helped set the city on the path to what a lot of people call sprawl, but which I prefer to see as a distributed network. Los Angeles may be difficult to grasp for people used to a stereotypical city with an obvious center, but if you appreciate a challenge, it may be your kind of town. Proteus was hard to get a hold of too, but there were rewards if you could manage it.

Gradually, the bars came off the windows and the paint became newer, the graphic design on the signs more up to date. The traffic got even worse. Temporary walls hid the construction of new buildings. The Hollywood Hills in the distance grew closer and more clearly defined. Soon I was passing storefronts promising the latest European furniture, and clothing stores that confined the word "boutique" to their names' subtitles. Gloria's Boutique was many blocks ago. Here I passed Closet Wise, A Sustainable Boutique. The check cashing establishments gave way to bank branches.

I turned on Willoughby Avenue, which made me think of Jane Austen and that cad who takes advantage of silly, hyper-romantic Marianne Dashwood. I wondered if whoever named the street had that in mind. Probably not. Some guy probably just named it after himself. I'd like to think people have more imagination than that, but I find they rarely do. There was a vintage clothing store on the corner, and the buildings on the adjoining streets were a mix of small houses and warehouses, except for one that loomed over the rest like a middle schooler who was first in his class to have a growth spurt. That turned out to be my destination, 954 Persimmon Way.

I wondered how long Bob and Harvey's business had been in that building. It was ten stories of heavy concrete and smallish windows, and it was old enough to have no parking structure or underground parking, just a ground level lot, which luckily for me was far from full. I saw no attendant or kiosk or any indication I had to pay. I parked, put my reflective sun-blocking screen up behind the windshield, got out, and walked over to the entrance, making sure I heard that comforting beep that assured me that my car was locked. According to my phone the time was 10:36.

A car drove by blasting California Girls, the original Beach Boys version. I half-expected it to be one of those old wood-panelled station wagons, or a VW van with flowers painted on it, but it was an ordinary black SUV. As the music faded away, I opened the glass double doors leading to what may forty or so years ago have been a fashionably decorated lobby, but was now a decaying cavern lined in scratched mirrored surfaces and dusty filigree. The light fixtures were wide cylinders hanging vertically from the ceiling by narrow cables, like cans on strings. Their circles of light made giant polka dots on the shiny floor and the vinyl-covered armchairs that were scattered about. The most prevalent color was that peculiar orange, a little less red than canned tomato soup, that had a surprising era of popularity once, a phenomenon which could be related to that era's reputation for widespread experimentation with drugs. At least, that was the best explanation I could think of.

There was not a single human being in the whole expanse of the room. I was tempted to shout across it to test for an echo, but the possibility that there could be some unseen person nearby who might hear me held me back. There was a long desk to my right with capital letters across the front spelling "INFORMATIO". I checked behind it, just in case there was someone there, or maybe the missing "N", but no such luck. The "N" seemed to have made good its escape, and I was beginning to think it had the right idea.

I headed toward the elevators, although the more I looked around at the general state of disrepair, the less unappealing the prospect of walking up eight flights of stairs became. I walked all the way to them, at the back of the room, hearing only the click of my heels on the floor. I was relieved when the button on the wall immediately lit up, and even more when the elevator car arrived without noticeable squeaking or sounds of straining cables. The doors opened smoothly, and I decided to chance it, crossing my fingers just in case that might make a difference. I hit the 9 button and went up.

The elevator shuddered but served its purpose, and soon the doors opened on an empty hallway painted that same orange color that infested the lobby. The carpet was a paisley pattern of the same color mixed with brown. The brown didn't help. On the wall in front of me was a gold plaque that indicated that offices 910-930 were to my right, so I walked that way. Soon the hallway ended in a T at another hallway with another plaque. This one informed me that offices 910-920 were to my left, so I turned that direction.

I saw two people in the hallway. One was a short, dumpy, balding man in a baggy blue suit, puffing along toward me and intermittently wiping his forehead and upper lip with a white handkerchief. Between him and me was a middle-aged woman with a bright blond cloud of hair, a blouse, skirt, and pumps in varying shades of beige, and two vivid patterned scarves folded into broad triangles, one at her neck and one at her waist. The bright red and green and blue of her scarves against the orange of the walls and carpet nearly made me dizzy. She was standing in front of door 914, pounding on it with her right fist.

"Harvey!" she yelled, "Let me in! I know you're in there!" She pounded a few more times. "Harvey!"

The dumpy man, whom I now suspected to be Bob, rushed over to her and shushed her. In the process of doing so, he saw me.

"Ms. Graepenteck?" he asked, pronouncing it correctly this time. He wiped his face again and retired the handkerchief to his pocket.

"Ella."

"Nice to meet you." He took a few steps toward me so he could shake my hand. "This is Barbara Milvander. Barbara, this is Ella Graepenteck, a new customer."

Barbara turned and saw me. The look on her face changed from frustration to forced graciousness as she put out her hand. I shook it.

"This must look strange," she said, "it's just that Harvey..."

"Harvey must have just stepped out," Bob said as he fiddled anxiously with his keys. He found the right one and, with just the slightest hesitation, unlocked the door. He opened it, and Barbara charged inside, adjusting her hair and scarves and then heading for an open door to the left.

"Harvey is my partner," Bob reminded me as he guided me toward a similar door to the right, "Harvey Wilmette." The office seemed to consist of three rooms, Harvey's office, Bob's office, and the reception area. Harvey's office door was behind a high counter where a receptionist would sit, if there were one, and Bob's was between two armchairs, upholstered in imitation leather the exact yellowish color of the palomino model horses I had as a child. That thought put unsettling images in my head, but I ignored them. The carpet was thin and tan, making me think of obvious jokes about aspiring actresses, and the walls were a dingy off-white. The fluorescent ceiling lights were on and slightly buzzing. At least nothing in there was orange.

Before we made it to his office door, Bob and I both turned our heads to the left because of a sound Barbara made, a loud, sharp, gasp. It was followed very quickly by an even louder sustained scream.

We both moved closer to her, edging toward the back of the reception room so we could see around the counter, as she continued to scream. There was something at her feet, in Harvey's office doorway. It was the top of a man's head, with very little hair. The head was attached to a thin body in a very worn blue suit, and the carpet around it was soaked in dark red blood.

Chapter 3: Harvey Wilmette

I had never seen a dead body before. I don't know if Bob or Barbara had or not, but it didn't seem like it. Barbara was just standing there screaming, getting blood on her beige pumps. Bob collapsed into one of the palomino armchairs, sweating and staring. He didn't even get out his handkerchief. My immediate reaction was a full body shiver, and then I started pacing in circles, tossing my arms about as if I were trying to shake off something that was stuck to my hands. The three of us created a ridiculous tableau.

Bob was the first one to say something sensible.

"We should call 911."

That was enough to knock me out of my pacing loop. I moved toward Barbara and managed to touch her arm without stepping in the blood. My touch seemed to turn her screaming to crying. She collapsed onto me, and I was able to pull her away from the body. I considered feeling for a pulse, but the man looked more like a discarded mannequin than an actual person. His skin looked almost plastic, and the blood on and around him looked anything but fresh. Besides, the thought of touching him made me want to start flopping my arms around again, and if I did that I would drop Barbara.

A tall man in a grey suit appeared in the open hall doorway, apparently from one of the nearby offices, with a questioning look on his face.

"Call 911," I said, as calmly as I could. "Someone's dead."

The man's thick eyebrows shot up closer to his carefully tended hairline, but he reached into his pocket and pulled out his phone. A few other people appeared in the doorway, but no one came in.

I eased Barbara out of the blood and then out of her shoes and into the empty armchair. She was still crying, but her sobs had become quieter. I was still shaking. I wondered if that was a symptom of shock. There was no place else to sit in the reception area, so I went into Bob's office and sat in one of the two ladder-backed wooden chairs in front of his desk. I tried to focus on taking deep breaths.

The name Edmund Walforth appeared in my peripheral vision, so I turned my head toward it, still concentrating on breathing. It was on the top document of a pile on Bob's desk. He must have gathered materials together in preparation for our meeting. I knew I probably shouldn't move anything, but I didn't see how it would hurt for me to read a few documents while we were waiting for the police. Besides, I couldn't remember ever needing a distraction more desperately than at that moment.

The document that had caught my eye was some kind of employment record from California Pictures. I learned that Edmund Walforth was making $120 a week in 1926, which was probably a lot. The real gold, though, was three pages down in the pile. It was a faded carbon copy, so faded that it wasn't clear what exactly the document was, but I was able to make out the name Edmund Walforth and a date of birth, 12 August 1893. I got out the notebook I always carry with me and wrote that down, and when I looked at the carbon copy again I saw another name, Ezekiel Wilder. I could hear people coming into the outer office, probably the police. I wrote down that name too and put the papers I'd looked at back on the pile they came from.

A uniformed police officer poked his head into Bob's office and asked me to come out. Bob and Barbara and I were guided out into the hallway. The bystanders had been pushed back, and there were paramedics there who checked to make sure we were okay. The man on the floor was officially declared to be Harvey Wilmette, and he was professionally diagnosed as seriously and definitively dead.

Soon two policemen in suits rather than uniforms appeared. They looked exactly like actors playing homicide detectives in a movie. One was medium height, with greying hair, brown eyes, and a little bit of a paunch, but still looking fit. He turned out to be Detective Rafael Vasquez. The other was younger and taller, broad-shouldered, with slightly wavy, very dark hair. He was Detective Cormac Roth.

The tall man who called 911 was the tenant in the office next door, number 912, which he was letting the police use as a sort of temporary command center. That is where the detectives questioned us. The nameplate on the door said Richard Halberford, CPA, so I assumed that was the tall man's name and profession. The layout, carpet and walls in 912 were the same as in 914. Detective Vasquez talked to Barbara in the room behind the reception counter, while Detective Roth talked to Bob in the other one. I was instructed to wait in the reception area in one of four chairs made of black vinyl stretched on metal frames. I sat there, wrapped in the shiny blanket the paramedics had given me, no longer shaking, waiting my turn.

To distract myself some more and to pass the time, I got out my phone and opened the app for my favorite genealogy website. I searched for an Ezekiel Wilder born in the US in 1893. The results loaded slowly, but I wasn't exactly in a rush. Eventually words started appearing in what had been blank space, and right at the top of the list was an entry from a collection called U.S. Select Births and Christenings 1867-1931. It showed an Ezekiel Wilder born 12 August 1893 in Nebraska. I checked my notebook to be sure I had remembered correctly. I had. Edmund Walforth's date of birth was 12 August 1893. This was way too easy.

Detective Roth came out of the inner office and looked at me, so I put my phone and notebook away. He sat down in the chair next to mine, his notepad out, a pen in his hand. He smelled nice, not like cologne, just like a clean man, with hints of soap and shampoo.

He asked me to spell my name and to give him my address and phone number, so I did. His eyes had brown and green in them, hazel eyes. I found myself wondering about the etymology of the word hazel, an odd word, really, and then whether or not Detective Roth liked hazelnuts. His eyes were mostly green around the pupils, but more brown around the edges. They were soft eyes, but the look in them was sharp, suspicious, an appropriate look for a detective.

"Can you take me through your morning, where you were, what you did?"

"I woke up about 6:30, went for a short jog around the neighborhood, came back around 7:00 and had breakfast and a shower, checked emails and the news. Around 9:45 I left the house to come here. I had an appointment with Mr. Ogilvie at 10:30."

"Was there anyone with you, any of that time?" His eyes went down to his notebook while he asked that.

"No. I was alone."

His eyes came back to mine. "Did you make or receive any phone calls?"

"Mr. Ogilvie called me about 10:15 to tell me he was running late."

"Anything else?"

"No other phone calls. I sent some emails before I left the house."

"Had you met Mr. Ogilvie before?"

"I'd never even spoken to him before that phone call. We had only exchanged emails."

"Why were you meeting today?"

"I have a client... I'm a genealogist, and I have a client who I believe is related to a minor 1920s moviestar. Mr. Ogilvie has a lot of information about 1920s moviestars."

"So it was purely a business meeting?"

"Yes."

"Had you ever met Barbara Milvander or Harvey Wilmette before today?"

"No."

"Can you describe for me what happened here this morning, when you arrived?"

I did, in detail. I told him the time my phone said I arrived, and that I was relieved the elevator worked. I recounted everything I heard anyone say. I mimed pounding on the door when I told him how Barbara Milvander was yelling for Harvey, and I demonstrated exactly how I pulled her away from the blood. I told the detective absolutely everything except the part about my going through Bob's papers and taking notes. It wasn't that there was anything necessarily wrong with that. It just didn't seem like something he needed to know.

Detective Roth finished writing on his notepad and looked me in the eye again. The sharpness in his expression had decreased substantially.

I don't know why, but I blurted out, "I've never seen a dead body before."

The detective's cheeks tightened, as if he were trying to suppress a smile. "Well, you are keeping your composure very well."

I shook my head. "You didn't see me when I first saw it, I mean him."

"It's a tough thing to see."

"He looked so small, so fragile. I'd never seen him before, so maybe he always looked like that, but for some reason I doubt it."

The detective seemed to be waiting for me to continue, but I couldn't think of anything else to say. After a minute or so he stopped waiting.

"Thank you Ms. Graepenteck. We may need to ask you more questions at a later time, but you can leave now if you wish. Would you like me to have an officer take you home?"

"No, I'm all right."

He handed me his card and asked me to call him if I remembered anything else. His hands looked strong, and his fingernails were as clean as the rest of him. As I stood up, I inexplicably blurted out something else.

"A tattered coat upon a stick."

"A what?"

"It's a line from a poem. Yeats. It's what Harvey Wilmette looked like, lying there."

The detective looked perplexed. I rebuked myself internally. What a ridiculous, pompous thing to say. Who goes around quoting Yeats? Where did that come from? I turned to go, leaving the shiny blanket on the chair, and tried to imagine I hadn't said anything.

As I walked through the now crowded hallway and lobby and back to my car, my focus shifted from my embarrassment to the memory of all that blood, on Mr. Wilmette's head and the carpet and Ms. Milvander's shoes. I also kept thinking about hazel, the color, the tree, the nut, the detective's eyes. I even thought about Ezekiel Wilder, and how his name shared letters with hazel and Wilmette. Trauma and shock can really jumble things up in a person's head. I turned the radio up loud and drove home.

Chapter 4: 2317 Cedar Hill Avenue

My little sanctuary, at 2317 Cedar Hill Avenue, is one of the few bungalows left in what was once an all bungalow neighborhood in Santa Monica, next to the airport. Many of my neighbors have filled their lots to the edges with extensions to their houses and garages, making it hard to avoid looking in each other's windows. Some of them have put in pools. My house still has just the two small bedrooms and one and a half baths it originally had. I use the second bedroom as an office.

I have a small, one car garage that houses my little Fiat with room to spare. I bought the car because it is tiny and easy to park almost anywhere. It is also undeniably adorable, and that and its cheerful light blue color tend to lighten my mood whenever I see it, even, a little bit, when I came out of 954 Persimmon Way having just seen a dead body and been questioned as part of a murder investigation.

The cheerful color wasn't nearly enough to erase the thoughts and images of that morning from my mind, and neither was the loud music I listened to on my drive home, but both helped a little. I could feel my shoulders relax somewhat as I turned into the alley behind my house, officially a street called Cedar Hill Place. The garage is separate from the house and opens onto the alley. Both the garage and the house are painted a color called Sunwash. It straddles the border between off-white and pale yellow, which may sound like it looks like old paper, but it actually makes the walls look like they are lit by the sun all the time. I don't know what brilliant collaboration of artistry and chemistry created it, but the moment I saw it I knew it was the color I wanted for my house.

That day it was even more of a relief than usual to turn down that alley, open the Sunwash colored garage door, and park. After turning off the car I just sat in it for a moment, breathing. Then I got out, closed the garage door, and opened the little door that leads to my backyard, an oasis surrounded by a six foot tall brick wall that connects the house to the garage and shields me from having to see what my neighbors are doing.

The yard had once been an expanse of green lawn with a path of paving stones from the little door in the garage to the back door of the house, but the path is all that is left of the original landscaping. I long ago converted from grass to native succulents, doing my part for water conservation while simultaneously eliminating almost all need for tending. I get to be responsible and lazy at the same time. It's win-win.

I had walked about halfway down the path when I felt compelled to go back to the garage to make sure I had locked the car and all the windows were up. I had, and they were. I closed and locked the door to the garage again and turned back to the house. This time I made it all the way there. I unlocked the door, went in, and closed and locked it behind me. I heard my mother's voice in my head, telling me I really should have an alarm system installed, but I dismissed it. I put down my purse and took off my shoes as usual, but then I found myself walking all over the house, making sure all the doors and windows were closed and locked. I looked into every closet, under the bed, every place a person could hide.

Finally, I collapsed on my overstuffed grass green sofa and berated myself for being paranoid. There was no logical reason anyone would be after me. It was pure chance that I happened to go to that office on the day someone was found murdered there. I knew nothing about

Harvey Wilmette or the circumstances surrounding his death. I was no threat to anybody. I'd had a shocking experience that was generating irrational fears. While driving home, I had even thought a particular blue car was following me, but that was obviously my imagination getting overexcited and playing tricks. I had no reason to be afraid. I said, out loud, "Stop it! Just stop it!" When you live alone, you can do things like that. My brief outburst actually made me feel a bit better. I took a shower, made some hot chocolate, and turned on the TV. I pulled up Netflix and decided to rewatch old episodes of Poirot.

After just a few minutes I paused Poirot because I heard my phone ringing from my purse. I got up to get it.

"Hi Aunt Agatha!" She is actually my great aunt, but who calls a person Great Aunt Agatha?

"Hello Ella! I'm so glad you picked up. How are you?"

I didn't want to dampen the mood with talk of dead bodies, so I just trotted out the appropriate pleasantries.

"Ella, I have a question for you."

"Yes?"

"What was the name of Harriet's first husband, the one from Chicago?"

"Alfred Eliot Reynolds."

"That's right. I knew you would know right away, and what year did they get married?"

"I'm pretty sure it was 1898. Let me check for you."

"Thank you so much, Ella. It WAS Reynolds, Alfred Eliot Reynolds."

That last part wasn't said to me. She was evidently in mid-conversation with someone. I paid only half attention while I got out my laptop and opened up my files on my family.

The Harriet we were discussing was Aunt Agatha's aunt Henrietta Eylerbetz. Harriet was the nickname she went by. She was the youngest of six children of Edward Eylerbetz, a traveling salesman who moved in the 1860s from what is now Germany to what is now Canada, where he met and married his wife Augusta. They had their children in various parts of what is now Michigan. Their oldest daughter, Violet, Aunt Agatha's mother and my great grandmother, was born in a little town in the Upper Peninsula in 1875. My middle name is Violet after her. When Edward died in 1886, the family moved to Detroit, and later to Chicago, where all three Eylerbetz brothers eventually made their living as portrait artists.

Harriet was by far the wildest Eylerbetz child. At the age of 16 she eloped with the scion of a wealthy Chicago political family, the aforementioned Alfred Eliot Reynolds. It was a huge scandal. My favorite headline is from the Chicago Herald: Runaway Reynolds Romance. Alfred's mother apparently fainted at the news. Harriet and Alfred ran off to Los Angeles, where it seems he spent most of his time drinking and gambling his money away.

"Yes, it was July 15th, 1898."

"1898. Yes, thank you Ella. My friend here knows the Reynolds family. Isn't that amazing?"

"Small world."

"It really is. Thank you so much!"

"You're very welcome."

I unpaused Poirot, but I couldn't concentrate on it. I was thinking too much about real death to pay attention to a fake one.

There was a sudden death that had affected Harriet and Alfred Reynolds, in 1901. The middle Eylerbetz sister, Agatha, after whom Aunt Agatha was named, was killed by an automobile as she crossed a street. It was an accident, not a murder, but it was quite a shock. It brought Harriet back to Chicago, and everyone more or less back to their senses. Harriet and Alfred got quietly divorced.

Soon after that, the eldest Eylerbetz brother, Edward Jr., moved to New York City, where he continued to find success as a painter. His mother and brothers eventually followed him there, but not until around 1910. In the meantime, Frederick and Ulysses, the other brothers, continued to be part of the Chicago art scene, and from 1903-1905, Violet Eylerbetz followed her brothers' path as a student at the renowned Chicago Art Institute.

Harriet went with Edward Jr. to New York and managed to get bit parts in early silent movies as the actress Harriet Rush. She didn't find stardom, but in 1904 she did find another wealthy husband, producer Lester Hodelman, and in 1906 they had their son Lester Jr., who later became the actor Reginald Ellis, friend of Edmund Walforth, who it seemed was actually Ezekiel Wilder of Nebraska. In 1908, Lester Sr.'s company changed its name from Royal Productions to California Pictures and became one of the first movie studios to move west, so Harriet found herself back in Los Angeles. Alfred Eliot Reynolds had gone broke and slunk home to Chicago by then.

Both Harriet and Violet were very beautiful, in exactly the way that was most appreciated at the time, torrents of dark hair, skin like undyed silk, faces and bodies that were all slope and curve. Publicity photos of Harriet Rush are stunning, and Aunt Louisa, my grandfather's other sister, besides Aunt Agatha, has a portrait of Violet that will make you forget to breathe. There are probably other portraits, scattered among various relatives. I imagine Violet and her brothers all painted each other for practice.

It was around that same time, 1908, that Violet met Heinrich Graepenteck. He grew up on a farm in Bavaria and somehow ended up in Chicago, working as a day laborer. They married in 1909 and came to California. I suspect the Hodelmans orchestrated some sort of opportunity for them, but I haven't yet discovered what it was.

Lester Hodelman Sr. was an influential man. He probably had all kinds of connections. I wondered if he could get a name put on a birth certificate that wasn't the person's legal name. Would that have been difficult to do in 1926? That thought made me curious again about Ezekiel Wilder.

I noted the time, almost 3:00, because I was about to start doing work for which I get paid by the hour. I went to my favorite genealogy website and started a private tree for Ezekiel Wilder, born 12 August 1893 in Nebraska. A general search brought up the birth index I had seen before, and a number of other records. I clicked on a listing from the 1900 U.S. federal census and looked at the scanned image of the census page. It showed the family of James Wilder, a farmer, living with his wife, eight children, and his widowed mother. One of the children was a boy named Ezekiel, and his birth date was given as August 1893. That was probably him, but I couldn't be certain. I attached the record to the tree, so I wouldn't lose track of it. I also attached the birth index record.

I found the Wilder family living in the same place on the 1910 census, and Ezekiel was not listed with them. That was promising. Maybe he'd gone to California already by then. I found a listing for an Ezakeel Wilder, born 1892 in Nebraska, in Los Angeles in 1910. He was a waiter. That was even more promising. Census records are full of bad spelling and inaccurate birth data, so the slight differences didn't discourage me.

I found him again in the 1920 census, but his was the last line on the page, and most of it was illegible. I could make out his name and age, but that was about it. Those old records are all handwritten, and sometimes there are smudged bits, or places where ink spilled, or frayed edges. Sometimes you get lucky and find pages written by a tidy person with impressive penmanship, but more often deciphering the writing takes significant effort.

I couldn't find Ezekiel in 1930. That was promising too, because if he was Edmund Walforth his name would have been changed by then, but it was hardly definitive. In genealogy you always have to keep in mind the old aphorism that absence of evidence is not evidence of absence.

I took another look at the 1920 census page. It was still just as illegible. I realized, though, that I hadn't done something I always do when I find someone at the bottom of a page, which is to look at the top of the next page. Ezekiel was listed as a lodger in a boarding house, and as he wasn't with any of his family in 1910, I didn't expect him to be with any of them in 1920, but I looked anyway, and I was glad I did. The person at the top of the next page was another lodger by the name of Isaac Wilder, born 1898 in Nebraska. I looked at the James Wilder family in 1900 and in 1910, and sure enough, there was an Isaac of the right age in both lists. I looked for the James Wilder family in Nebraska in 1920. James was dead by then, but his widow Elizabeth was still living with several of the children, and neither Ezekiel nor Isaac was among them. This was beginning to look more definitive.

All of a sudden I was very, very hungry. I realized I hadn't eaten since breakfast. I checked the time. It was 4:02. Not bad for an hour's work. I closed my laptop and looked up at the TV. Poirot was just about to board a riverboat and cruise along the Nile. This was one of my favorite episodes. I hit the pause button and went to the kitchen to get something to eat.

Chapter 5: Sara Markis Plus One

Ezekiel Wilder's brother Isaac proved easy to track. He had stayed in Los Angeles, worked as an office clerk, married, and then had a son named Isaac Jr. who grew up to be a lawyer. Isaac Sr. died in 1974, but I couldn't find a death record for Isaac Jr., so he was probably still alive, and if so, very likely still in L.A. If Sara wanted to, she could try to find him. Maybe he or someone in his family would be willing to do a DNA test, to see if Sara's grandmother was really Ezekiel/Edmund's daughter. The Wilder family might also know more about Ezekiel and his life. I would give my client the information, and then it would be up to her. That sort of thing is outside my area of expertise. I'm no private eye. I track down records, not people.

By Wednesday I had used up the ten hours Sara Markis had paid for, and it had been almost a week since we had last spoken. I felt I had to tell her what had happened at Bob Ogilvie's office on Monday, to explain why I hadn't obtained more information there, so I called her. She was shocked and sympathetic. I told her I had prepared a preliminary report, and we agreed to meet on Friday at her apartment so I could explain it to her and answer any questions.

It was quiet on Bluebird Avenue that Friday, but there were a lot of cars parked on the street. I had to go several blocks to find a space. I didn't mind the walk, though. The weather apps on my phone agreed the temperature was hovering around 72 degrees Fahrenheit, 22 Celsius, and it felt like they were right. A pleasant breeze kept redrawing the shadows the trees made on the sidewalk. The building's main entry door was unlocked, so I went in and up to the third floor. I knocked on the door of 3A, and Sara opened it almost immediately. Her hair was in a tight ponytail, and she was wearing a white T-shirt and jeans, both of the type that are intentionally "distressed" so that the wearer can pretend to want to look as if she is anti-establishment and impervious to the opinions of others. She was barefoot, and both her fingernails and toenails were perfectly painted a bright pink. Her makeup also looked expertly applied. Her hands were empty this time. I wondered where her phone was.

I was not surprised to see that she was not alone in the room. There was a man there. He was only a little older than Sara, medium height, brown hair, brown eyes. He was handsome, but not so much that he would stand out in the kind of L.A. crowd in which he looked like he'd want to be seen. I would bet he had been the best looking boy at his high school, but only the eighth or tenth best looking at college. He wore glasses with rectangular lenses and barely detectable rims. Like Sara, he was in jeans and a T-shirt, but he wasn't barefoot. He was wearing athletic shoes that were probably of some particularly fashionable type. I wouldn't know. I try to keep up on a lot of things, but which athletic shoe is the trendiest is not one of them.

Sara expressed herself as enthusiastically as she had the last time I was there.

"Hi again! Thanks for coming! Come on in! This is Andrew Cobb!"

The man stepped toward me and we shook hands.

"I hope you don't mind about Andrew joining us, but after what you said about what happened I was just kind of nervous and wanted someone here with me." She flashed him a smile, and he gave her a half smile back.

"Of course."

"Would you like some coffee, or tea, or anything?"

"No, thank you."

We all sat on the big white sofa, Sara between me and Andrew, and looked through my report.

"The evidence does seem to indicate that Ezekiel Wilder and Edmund Walforth were the same person, and the fact that Edmund Walforth doesn't seem to have existed until the mid-1920s is a good explanation for why you have been unable to find information about him before."

"Yes, wow, that makes a lot of sense, and this is a lot of information! I can't believe you found out so much in such a short time, especially after, you know, what happened. I mean, I just can't imagine, you know, how awful that must have been."

"It was unpleasant."

"Well, yeah, it must have been horrible! I mean, you just don't expect things like that to happen, I mean, just going to some office and then there's something like that. How just awful!"

"Well, it's over now, and some good came out of it. I did find out about Ezekiel Wilder."

"But I feel so bad about what you had to go through."

"That's kind of you, but there's no need for you to feel bad. I'm fine. Truly. So, I think your best bet for making sure this man is your great grandfather is to contact the

Wilder family and see if one of them will do a DNA test. That isn't the kind of work I do, but if you would like me to learn more about the Wilders, to go back further, either now or after you confirm you are related, I can do that."

Andrew Cobb spoke up for the first time. "I can help with contacting the Wilder family."

Sara looked up at him and smiled again. He looked at me and said, apparently by way of explanation, "I'm a lawyer." He looked pointedly into my eyes as he said that, his mouth the tiniest bit turned up at the corners, as if he planned to smile but was waiting for the right moment. It seemed I was supposed to be impressed. I decided to be polite.

"A lawyer! Great!"

He took that as his cue to smile and look down as if embarrassed, showing me how humble he was. Sara moved closer to him and smiled wider. I tried to make my face look as if I understood what she saw in him. If I wasn't doing a good job of it, neither of them seemed to notice.

"I certainly understand if you want to stop here, at least for now, to make sure he is your ancestor before you hire me to research the family further."

I thought I saw Andrew make a small movement. Did he squeeze Sara's hand?

"I think Sara wants to know more, don't you, Sara? The evidence seems pretty clear. Why wait?"

Sara moved her gaze from him to me. "I would like to know more, I mean, if you don't mind, after everything that happened."

"I don't mind at all. What happened had nothing to do with the research I was doing. I was just unlucky, to be there on that particular day."

"You are so strong! I don't think I could handle something like that." She leaned into Andrew's shoulder, and he put his arm around her.

It seemed like a good time for me to leave. I pulled a contract for ten more hours of genealogical research out of my bag and put it on the glass coffee table, next to the preliminary report. Sara signed the contract without reading it and wrote me another check. Her lawyer friend made no attempt to encourage greater circumspection on her part, making the terms "lawyer" and "friend" seem like inaccurate descriptors. Luckily for her, I am honest, at least in legal matters, and this contract was exactly the same as the one she had signed for the previous ten hours. In any case, it wasn't my place to criticize her choice of companions.

When the transaction was done, both Sara and Andrew stood up and walked me to the door. When I had one foot in the hallway and one still in the apartment, Sara took my hand.

"Thank you so much." She stood a little too close to me as she said it, her eyes very wide and staring directly into mine, her voice slowly drawing out the vowels of each word. Then she turned her face toward Andrew and stared into his eyes exactly the same way. I felt like I was watching a high school play.

I disentangled my hand from hers and said goodbye as I moved the lagging half of my body into the hall. I started walking away before the door was closed. Questions about the relationship between Sara and Andrew and why it would matter to him that she continue this research filled my head as I walked to my car, making me wish, not for the first time, that I wasn't so cursed with curiosity. If I had never taken this job, not only would I not have come across poor, murdered Harvey Wilmette, but I also wouldn't have met Andrew Cobb or had to witness the spectacle of his interaction with Sara Markis.

But all of that was none of my business. She was my client. Ten paid hours is ten paid hours, and I take pride in my work. She would get her money's worth, and whatever else might be going on in her life was not my concern. I got back in my cheerful light blue car and headed back to my Sunwash colored house.

Chapter 6: Dashing Edmund Walforth

Soon after I arrived home, my phone rang. It was Detective Roth. The flicker of excitement that I felt at the sound of his voice must have been curiosity about what happened to Harvey Wilmette. I didn't learn anything from the phone call, though.

"There have been some developments in the case, and we have more questions we would like to ask you. Could you come down to the station?"

"Right now?"

"If possible."

"Okay."

Aside from some discussion of logistics, that was about it. No matter how many times I replayed the conversation in my head, I could distill no more meaning from anything he said. I hoped I would be able to learn more in person. While driving there, I once again had the feeling I was being followed. I thought I saw the same dark blue car I had seen on Monday, but it was probably just a similar one. There are a lot of blue sedans on the freeways at any given moment. I scolded myself for giving in to paranoia.

The police station was a long, low, brick building with concrete on the roof and at the corners, and no windows. The front door was deeply recessed, about ten feet back from the outer wall. I couldn't see it until I was directly in front of it, and even then it was obscured by shadows. As I stepped toward it I felt my heartbeat quicken, probably a reaction from the most ancient parts of my brain, residue from ancestors' experiences entering caves and tunnels. I took a deep breath before I opened the door.

By contrast, the fluorescent lit, starkly white interior seemed almost inviting. I made sure to smile as I walked to the front desk and explained why I was there. A young woman in uniform, her dark hair pulled into a tight bun, let me through a door that led to a hallway that led to another police officer, this one a young man with a clean shaven face and very short hair, and another door. Through that door was a large room divided by a wall of glass. I wondered if the glass was bulletproof. There were uniformed officers on the near side of it and people in suits, including Detectives Vasquez and Roth, beyond it. There

46

was a glass door in the glass wall. Detective Vasquez made a gesture and an officer near the door opened it for me.

Detective Roth offered me coffee, which I declined. He seemed even taller than I remembered. Detective Vasquez invited me to sit across from him at his broad, gray desk, and then he started asking me questions.

"Have you seen or spoken with Robert Ogilvie or Barbara Milvander since the day you found the body?"

"No."

"Had you ever seen or spoken with either of them before that day?"

"No."

"Did either of them ever mention Harvey Wilmette's brother, James Wilmette?"

"No."

"What about James Wilmette's wife, Miranda Wilmette?"

"No."

"Take us again through every detail of your experience that morning, beginning with the phone call you received from Robert Ogilvie."

I did, and the detectives seemed satisfied. I asked about the developments in the case that Detective Roth had mentioned on the phone, and whether Harvey Wilmette's brother and his wife were suspects, but they wouldn't tell me anything. They just said it was an ongoing investigation.

They had made me even more curious, but I knew the best thing for me to do was to forget all about Harvey Wilmette and everything connected to him. The smartest and the safest course of action was just to let the police do their job, and stay out of it. Unfortunately, I am not too smart, and my record on safety is nothing to brag about.

I left the police station and found myself driving straight to the unusually tall building on Persimmon Way. It looked the same on Friday afternoon as it had on Monday morning. There was plenty of room in the parking lot. I didn't see any police cars. The glass double doors were unlocked, and the lobby looked just as shabby and just as empty.

I rode the elevator to the ninth floor, and the doors opened on the glaringly orange hallway. I turned right, and then left. The hallway was completely deserted, and all the doors were closed, including number 914. I knocked on it.

Someone was in there. I could hear movement. After a few seconds, the door opened, and I was face to face with

Bob Ogilvie, looking almost the same as he had when I last saw him, except sadder, and exhausted. I tried to sound warm and comforting.

"Hello. How are you?"

He seemed to be trying to place my face. I put out my hand.

"Ella Graepenteck, from..."

"Oh! Oh yes, of course, Ms. Graepenteck."

"Ella."

"Ella, thank you. Um, yes, um, come in."

He stepped back from the doorway and I walked in. It seemed the place was no longer an active crime scene. I didn't see any police tape, and Bob appeared to be the only person in the office. It was a mess. There were papers piled everywhere. Files had been pulled out of drawers, some of which were hanging open. Photographs and magazines were on the floor.

"I'm so sorry, Bob, about what happened."

"Oh, well, thank you. I'm sorry, that you had to see... I'm sorry you were here. I mean, that that was the day."

"Thank you. It looks like the police have finished looking around."

"Oh, yes. They were pretty thorough."

"Have they found out who it was?"

"You mean who..." he looked at the still bloodstained place on the floor where Harvey Wilmette had been, "um, no, not yet."

"Do they have suspects? I mean, have they told you anything about the investigation."

"Oh, they don't tell me anything." Bob collapsed into the same armchair he had collapsed into when he saw Harvey's body, in exactly the same way. I thought he might be about to cry.

"I'm sorry. I don't mean to upset you. I'm just curious, but I can go if I'm bothering you."

"Oh, no, stay. I'm just sorry, like I said, that you had to be here, had to see... Would you like a cup of tea?"

He looked lonely, as if he really wanted me to stay a while, or at least that was what I told myself. My curiosity makes me good at my job, but I've been told it can make me insensitive, and I know it can lead to poor decisions. I could feel myself about to make one.

"I would love a cup of tea. Thank you. That's very kind of you."

"Least I can do. You know, if you still want to know about that fellow, that actor..."

"Edmund Walforth."

"Yeah, if you still want to know about him, the information is still in my office. If you want to, you can go look around." He gestured toward his office, and my eyes followed his arm. I could see piles of paper on his desk, on shelves, on the floor. Sara Markis had, after all, paid for ten more hours. Sticking around and going through those papers would be just doing my job.

"Thank you, I think I would like to have a look."

"Go on in. I'll get the tea."

It didn't take me long to find the right piles of papers. I sat on the floor and sorted through them.

Edmund Walforth had been a handsome man, in the 1920s style, slicked back hair, narrow mustache. His hair appeared to be blond, or light brown. All the photos were black and white. He was holding a cigarette in most of them.

The gossip magazines reported rumored romances between him and a number of starlets whose names I didn't recognize. There were mentions I'd seen before of him and his friend Reginald Ellis out on the town. There was a photo of them together. Edmund was thirteen years older than Reginald, but he didn't look it. I could see how he got away with claiming to be 25 on Sara's grandmother's birth certificate, in 1926. Reginald/Lester would have been about 20 that year. Edmund/Ezekiel didn't look more than five years older. If people would believe it, it was true enough. That was the essence of Hollywood magic.

Bob came in with two mugs of tea. He handed me one, and I put it down on the floor next to me. Bob sat in one of the wooden chairs and held his mug in both hands.

"Is there information there that helps you?"

"There is. I appreciate your letting me look."

He took his left hand away from his mug long enough to make a gesture waving away my appreciation. "Oh no, it's nothing. I feel terrible that you... Well..."

"It must have been much worse for you."

Bob took a sip of tea.

"I knew Harvey since we were fifteen years old. Fifteen. That's almost fifty years ago."

I couldn't think of an appropriate response, so I just watched him take another sip.

"We started this business in 1976. It was a special year. It was the bicentennial. Of course you're too young to remember that."

"No I'm not."

"What? Of course you are."

"I was a little kid, but I remember people talking about it, and specials on TV. I remember bicentennial quarters."

"Oh, I'd forgotten about those. Well, you don't look old enough to remember."

"Thank you."

"I'll be 65 years old this year. Never imagined getting to be 65 years old."

He took another sip of tea. To be sociable, I took a sip of mine.

"He wasn't perfect, Harvey, not even very good, but I don't know why anyone would want to kill him. He did make people mad sometimes. Barbara, she was his girlfriend for ten years. He made her mad, all the time, but she wouldn't kill him. His brother, James, they didn't get along too well, but he wouldn't kill him either. Who would kill Harvey?"

He took another sip, staring straight ahead, at nothing. It seemed best not to interrupt his train of thought.

"Sometimes, when we were young, you understand, we... we did some business with some sort of shady people, not criminals, you know, exactly, but not the most upstanding citizens, but nobody ever tried to kill us. Now, for years, we are just old men with a little business, just to make a living, and we don't even deal with those shady people, not for a long time. I just don't get it."

He drained his mug.

"I'm gonna get some more tea. Do you want some more?"

"No, I'm fine, thanks."

He got up and left the room, and I looked down at the papers in front of me again. I picked up another magazine, this one from February 1927, and flipped through it. I saw Edmund Walforth's name and read the paragraph around it.

All Hollywood is saddened by the passing of one of its up and coming stars. Dashing Edmund Walforth has died at just twenty-six years of age, succumbing to a respiratory infection. He was due to begin filming "The Flame of the Klondike" with the lovely Mavis Wales next month. What might have been a long and brilliant career is now cut short.

He definitely wouldn't be in the 1930 census. He had died when Sara's grandmother was less than a year old. It was possible he hadn't meant to abandon her. It was possible her mother hadn't intended to give her up. I would have to check the information Sara had given me. Was the baby given up for adoption immediately after birth, or later? Maybe things would have been different if Edmund/ Ezekiel hadn't died.

I gulped down some of the tea, gathered up my purse and the mug and the magazine, and went out to the reception area, where I ran into Bob on his way back.

"May I make a copy of this?"

"Sure. Copier is right there." He pointed behind the reception counter.

To get to it I had to walk right past the bloodstain. I tried not to look down as I went by. I reached the copier and lifted the lid.

"You know what, you can just take it, take whatever you want, really. Least I can do."

"No. I just need a copy of this, and one other thing I saw before. If my client wants any of these documents or magazines I will send her to you to buy them. You still have a business, Bob."

He stopped with his mug halfway to his mouth, and stared at me for a moment.

"Thank you, Ella."

I smiled and turned back to the copier.

With copies of the obituary and the California Pictures document I'd seen the day of the murder, the one with the name Ezekiel Wilder and the birthdate, in my purse, I shook Bob's hand again and made my way back through the orange hall and the shaky elevator and the empty lobby to my car.

I hadn't learned much about the crime, but I had gotten useful information for my client. It was a good reminder. I am a genealogist, not a detective. I was a witness, not even to a murder, but to the discovery of a body, and that was it. I would leave the hunt for the murderer to the police, and stick to what I know.

Chapter 7: The House of de Brisay

It was getting to be evening, and it was Friday, so I went directly to my mother's house without going home first. I grew up in that house, and so did my mother, and so did her father. On that side of the family, I am a third generation only child.

The house was built by my great grandfather, Patrick de Brisay III. The family mythology, still perpetuated by many of my relatives, is that the de Brisays are descended from French aristocrats who escaped the guillotine, but that is bunk. It wasn't hard to trace the family back to the first Patrick de Brisay, my great great great grandfather. He was a poor Irishman who, like so many others, emigrated to the U.S. during the potato famine in the 1840s. I suppose it's possible the de Brisay name originally came from some Norman knight, but I haven't found any evidence of that, or that my ancestors were doing anything other than farming in Ireland when the French revolted. Patrick I made his way out to San Francisco in time to capitalize on the gold rush, not by prospecting himself, but by providing services to the prospectors. I'm not sure what those services were, but I suspect they were less than legal, or at any rate less than ethical. A lot of things were legal then that aren't now. He is listed on the 1860 census and in city directories as a hotel keeper. If that's all he was, he was miraculously good at it, because when he died in 1862 he left his children burdened with the weight of enormous bank accounts.

His son Patrick Jr. moved to Los Angeles, bought a lot of land, and had a lot of children, but still didn't quite manage to spend his share. When he died in 1893, the land and the leftover money got distributed among his children. Some of the land turned out to have oil on it. My branch of the family didn't have that particular luck, but Patrick III did get some nice real estate. He built what is now my mother's house in 1906, and his only child, Patrick IV, was born there. That was the end of the Patricks, because my grandfather had no sons, but he named my mother Patricia. There are still plenty of de Brisays around L.A., my mother's second cousins and their kids and grandkids, and some are unimaginably wealthy, but we barely know each other, a fact that causes me to shed not one single tear. I have nothing against the house, though.

I worked my way around the traffic on the grid streets, and then up into the precarious windings off Laurel Canyon Boulevard. The road became narrower and narrower, and once again I was grateful for my tiny car. The hill rose up steeply to my right, and dropped off frighteningly to my left, dotted with homes I'd be too scared to live in on both sides. It seems every year at least one of those cliffhanging dwellings ends up sliding down a canyon in a torrent of mud. Of course most of them don't, so I suppose the odds are pretty good, and those houses do have impressive views. Still, I was glad Patrick de Brisay III built on a flat space at the top of a hill, far from the canyon's edge.

I turned onto Alta Brea Crescent and worked my way all the way to the top. The view from up there is nearly overwhelming. Immediately below you are hills and canyons filled with trees, large and small structures popping up among them in impossible places. The trees are usually green or brown, depending on how much rain has recently fallen, but some defy the seasonlessness and take on autumn colors. Beyond the hills, the expanse of Los Angeles stretches past the horizon. You can see clusters of tall buildings rising up like cathedrals, and between them, many more buildings, where there are so many people, with so many, many cars.

The house is not visible from the road. There is just a tall iron gate in a taller stone wall. Trees of several varieties press against the wall from the inside and lean over it, as if there isn't enough room for them and they are being pushed out. Just inside the gate is a huge palm tree, not the tall skinny kind you always see in photos, but the squat kind with a trunk like a giant brown pineapple. It has long, wide fronds that extend all the way across the driveway. I punched the code in to open the gate, passed through the palm frond archway, and wound around the driveway to the house.

It is just two stories tall, but it was intended to look substantial, as if it could have withstood attacks by lance and catapult. It is not a place of dark corridors and secret passages, but it does have stone steps leading up to a wide front terrace, and a heavy wooden door in its smooth stone walls.

I used my key to get in and turned off the alarm. I locked up and turned the alarm back on.

"Mom?"

She was usually in this part of the house when I arrived, but I was early.

I walked through the entryway into the enormous front room. The sun made big bright rectangles on the parquet floor and the now pale Turkish carpet that covered most of it. Nearly a third of the back wall was taken up by the tall, deep fireplace that as a child I used as an imaginary dungeon for imaginary villains. The four armchairs around it were still upholstered in their original green velvet, their worn places making them look distinguished, as if they had a little grey hair at their temples. The end tables all had sets of coasters on them, different ones from around the world. When I was little they all had ashtrays on them too, although even then they were rarely used.

I continued through the room, past the double doors that led to the formal dining room and through the archway into the kitchen. No sign of her there. I opened the door next to the door to the cellar and went up the narrow back stairs.

"Mom?"

"I'm in here!"

She was in her study, lying across the pale blue chaise longue, her masses of red hair spilling over the back of it, reading a book entitled <u>The Learning Brain: How Neurotransmitters Affect Cognition</u>. Every inch of wall in this room, aside from the trim around the windows and doors, was covered in lacquered mahogany bookshelves, and they were all full. There were beautiful leather bound volumes that had been there since the house was built, and more recent hardcovers and paperbacks on almost every imaginable topic, although the bulk reflected my mother's two favorites, science and history. There was a long table in the middle of the room that served as a desk. There were piles of books on it, and some papers too. There were two armchairs near the far wall, similar to the green velvet ones downstairs, but upholstered in brown leather. They had been well used when my grandfather lived here, but not much since then. My mother preferred the chaise longue.

She placed a bookmark in the book and put it down. Then she got up and gave me a hug. I asked her if anything was new.

"Not really. How was the rest of your week?"

"Not as bad as the first part."

"How could it be? What a horrible thing. Have they solved it?"

"Not yet. They asked me to come to the police station today for more questions."

"Questions about what?"

"Mostly just more details, and to repeat my account of what I saw and heard. They asked me about the dead man's brother and his wife, and of course I didn't know they existed, so I don't think I was any help. The other detective did the questioning this time, the older one. Maybe they thought I would remember more if I had to tell it again to someone else."

"Did you?"

"No."

"Seems sort of pointless then."

"On a totally different topic, did you see that the Oxford English Dictionary has just recognized 'chaise lounge' as an acceptable term?"

"What? No!"

"They did."

"Abominable!"

"I know."

"It's a long chair. That's it. Just a long chair, in French. Not a lounge. Horrendous!"

"Yes, but now officially acceptable."

She sighed and shook her head. I nodded in solidarity.

She headed into the hallway and I followed her back to the kitchen. The first thing she did there was turn on all the lights, blurring the boundaries between the areas where the sun was shining and the places it couldn't reach. The light on the terra cotta floor tiles brought out the reddish tones in the granite countertops. She leaned over the sink and washed her hands. When she was done, I did the same.

"What about the project you were working on, that client?"

"I'm still working on it. I met with her this morning, actually."

"You've had a busy day."

"Yes. The meeting was a bit odd. She had a man there with her. He's a lawyer, and they both seemed to believe that made him able to protect her or find things out for her or in some way be of use."

"People believe all kinds of things."

"Exactly. She wrote me a check for ten more hours, though."

"Ten hours is ten hours."

"Yep."

She picked a bottle of wine from the small rack on the counter and set about uncorking it and pouring some into two glasses. I opened a cabinet and pulled out the shabbat candlesticks and two candles. I put the challah, which had been bought that morning from a bakery down the hill, on a plate my mother had inherited from her mother. We put the candles, the challah, and the wine glasses on the round oak table in the breakfast nook.

"You know something weird?"

"What?"

"Ever since the day I saw the body, I've had this feeling sometimes when I'm driving that I'm being followed."

She looked alarmed.

"I think it's some kind of paranoiac reaction. I don't think anyone's really following me. Why would they? I just feel suspicious of the cars around me, and relieved when they turn a different way or pass me and drive off."

"People react to trauma in many different ways."

"Right. It's just strange. I hope it stops soon."

"Are we ready?"

"Yes."

I lit the candles with a long, thin lighter made for exactly that purpose, and we both waved our hands three times over them. Together we performed an abbreviated version of the traditional blessings over the candles, wine, and bread, and then we hugged and said, "Shabbat shalom!"

It was far from orthodox. There are people who might take issue with our version of the sabbath ritual, but they weren't there to see us.

It was after my grandmother died that my mother became seriously interested in her Jewish roots. Then when my father died it seemed to become even more important to her. We had started out doing it properly, with books on Jewish customs open while we did it, but eventually we had evolved our own adaptation.

My grandmother Anna wasn't religious at all. She married Patrick de Brisay IV, who was at least nominally Catholic, and she didn't keep shabbat or belong to a synagogue. The de Brisay family was not at all pleased when Patrick married a Jew, religious or not. They put a lot of pressure on his father to disinherit him, but to his credit, Patrick III resisted. I think he really liked my grandmother. I don't know that she would have understood this modified shabbat practice of ours, but I'm pretty sure she wouldn't have minded it either.

We ordered Thai food for dinner. While we were waiting for it, we turned on the TV in the kitchen and caught a telenovela. My mother likes to watch them to keep up on her Spanish. We yelled at the characters every time they did something stupid, which meant we were yelling most of the time.

I felt good on the drive home, more relaxed than I had been all week, since I had first seen Harvey Wilmette's body. I didn't even suspect the cars behind me of following me.

Chapter 8: An Attempt at Making Sense

I had absolutely no obligations that weekend, so I dedicated all my energies to avoiding activity of any useful kind. I spent most of my time lounging around the house in pajamas or sweats, reading mystery novels and watching television. There was something, though, that kept nagging at me. I knew the name Wilmette from somewhere, from before, and I couldn't remember where. It didn't strike me as a particularly rare name. I could have heard it any number of places, but I couldn't think of any.

Eventually, my resistance to productivity was overcome by my curiosity. I googled it. All I found was listing after listing about a town in Illinois.

I decided to go on my favorite genealogy website and see if I could find Harvey Wilmette's family. It didn't take long.

I found a birth record for Harvey Louis Wilmette, born 1951 in Los Angeles. His father was Louis Anthony Wilmette Jr., born 1926 in Los Angeles. I found Louis in

L.A. on the 1930 and 1940 U.S. censuses. His father, Louis Anthony Sr., was born about 1881 in Wisconsin. Then it hit me.

I went to my files on my great grandmother Violet Eylerbetz Graepenteck and her family. It was as I remembered. Among the artists at the Chicago Art Institute from 1903 to 1905, when Violet and her brothers were spending so much time there, was Louis A. Wilmette, from Wisconsin. If Louis had any claim to fame, it was as the best friend of F. H. (Francis Herbert) Rutledge, the painter of impressionistic prairie landscapes and some famous portraits, including one of Teddy Roosevelt. Rutledge was also at the Institute at that time. He went on to have a long life of artistic and material success, but also personal tragedies, including the early deaths of both his children. Long before he died, he had no family left to name in his will. He left specific paintings to several museums, and a hunk of money to the Chicago Art Institute, but the rest of his estate all went to Louis A. Wilmette.

I found this discovery disconcerting. It was strange enough that the ancestor my client was looking for had a connection to my own family. Now a man who had information about that ancestor in his office, who was found murdered the day I went there, turned out to be connected to the same branch of my family in a different way. It seemed like there should be a reason for that, but I couldn't think of one. It didn't make any sense, and that made me even more nervous than the coincidence did.

I couldn't stop trying to organize and categorize all the information in my head, but I also couldn't keep track of all the names and connections, so I decided to draw the problem, to write it all down. If I could lay it all out visually, maybe it would start to make sense. I would need a big piece of paper.

I went through the closet in the second bedroom, where I keep my office supplies, and discovered three pieces of white posterboard left over from some long forgotten project. That would do very well. I pulled one piece out, grabbed a marker, and headed to the kitchen, where there was a wide enough expanse of floor with no carpet. I lay the posterboard down on the floor and knelt at one of the long sides.

Near the bottom edge of the paper, in the middle, I wrote the name Harvey Wilmette. I drew a straight line up from him, and at the top of it I wrote Louis Wilmette Jr. Above him I drew another line and wrote Louis Wilmette

Sr. Well to the left of Harvey Wilmette, near the left edge of the paper, I wrote Bob Ogilvie. Between those two names, and a little above them, I wrote Edmund Walforth/Ezekiel Wilder. I drew a dotted line from him to the very bottom of the page and wrote Sara Markis. Just to the left of Edmund/Ezekiel, I wrote Reginald Ellis/Lester Hodelman Jr. I drew a line up from him and wrote the names Lester Hodelman Sr. and Harriet Eylerbetz at the top of it.

I sat back on my heels and looked at what I had. Who else did I know of who was connected to Harvey Wilmette? There was his brother James, and his wife. What was her name? The detectives had mentioned it. I started to write James Wilmette to the right of Harvey and then I remembered it. Miranda. I wrote James & Miranda Wilmette and drew a line from James up to Louis Wilmette Jr., so Harvey and James were both connected to their father. I thought Barbara Milvander should be somewhere on the page too. I had met her with Bob Ogilvie, so maybe I should put her near him, but she was Harvey Wilmette's girlfriend. I put her to Harvey's immediate left.

My doorbell rang. I considered getting up to answer it, but as I thought through the possibilities of who might be at my door, on a Sunday evening, without calling first, I felt my motivation shrinking. I stared at my posterboard diagram, unable to concentrate on it because I was listening for the doorbell to ring again. It didn't. Instead, there was the scratching, clicking sound of someone hanging an advertisement on my doorknob. I felt validated, justified in my antisocial laziness, and able to concentrate again.

I turned to Sara Markis. I thought I should include her lawyer friend. She certainly seemed to think he was important. I wrote Andrew Cobb to the left of her name. About halfway up the dotted line between Sara and Edmund Walforth, I wrote in Sara's grandmother, Lily/Emily, and above that her mother, Sara's great grandmother, Ellen Marie Walsh. I considered putting in Sara's parents, but it seemed unlikely they would prove important to the puzzle. Lily/Emily's adoptive parents might be worth considering, but I couldn't remember their names and I didn't want to get up to go look them up, so I just drew a line up from Lily/Emily and put a question mark at the top of it. I was satisfied I had all the pertinent people. Now it was time to draw their connections to me. I was already running out of space, but I was just going to have to cram more names in.

I went back to the left side of the paper where Harriet Eylerbetz sat above her son Reginald/Lester. From Harriet I drew a line up and squeezed in Edward & Augusta Eylerbetz at the top of it. From them I extended three other lines, for their children Violet, Frederick, and Ulysses Eylerbetz. After a moment I decided to add two more lines for their two other children. Even though Agatha died in 1901 and Edward Jr. moved to New York soon after, they might figure into the puzzle. I managed to keep the names Violet, Frederick, and Ulysses more or less on the same line with Louis Wilmette Sr. To the right of Louis I wrote F.H. Rutledge. Now all those artists who were together at the Chicago Art Institute were together on the posterboard.

Next to Violet's name I wrote Heinrich Graepenteck. From them I drew three lines, for their children Agatha, Louisa, and Henry. Next to Henry I wrote Mary Terence, my grandmother, and from them a line down, where I wrote Roland Henry Graepenteck, and next to him Patricia de Brisay, and a line down from them to Ella Violet Graepenteck. That put me at the bottom, near Sara Markis. I sat back on my heels again and looked at my work.

It just looked like a bunch of lines and names, some of them hard to read because I had to work so hard to squeeze them into small spaces. The whole undertaking seemed like a waste of time and posterboard. I still couldn't get my brain to process how both a murder victim and the client who had been the reason I crossed paths with him would have connections to the same branch of my family, and different kinds of connections. Sara, if she was really the descendant of Edmund Walforth, was connected to the Eylerbetzes through the 1920s movie business in L.A., and Harvey Wilmette was connected to them through the 1900s art world in Chicago. I couldn't get the pieces to connect.

I did notice something else, though. Although there were several people on the posterboard who had been at least a little famous at some point, there was only one who was still famous now: F.H. Rutledge. What if Louis Wilmette had inherited something of great value, something as yet not widely known? Maybe there was something that wasn't particularly valuable just after Rutledge died, but would be now. Maybe it was forgotten about, long overlooked. What if Harvey and his brother James had found and seen the potential of that previously unknown highly valuable thing? What if the murder had nothing to do with Harvey's current business, but was instead to do with his grandfather's connection to one of the most famous artists of the twentieth century?

It was a whole other realm of possible motives, and it seemed like something that might be helpful to the police. Detective Roth's card was still in my purse. It didn't seem worth bothering him with on a Sunday night, but in the morning I would call.

I was thirsty, and my knees hurt. I got up off the kitchen floor and poured myself a glass of water. As I was drinking it, I remembered the doorknob. The thought that whatever had been put on it might not be just an ad for a local restaurant or real estate agent, but something that would help me figure things out, tried to sneak its way to the forefront of my mind. If I were the main character in a TV show, whatever was on the doorknob would turn out to be something important, a clue. I knew it was silly, but I put down my glass of water and eagerly went to open the front door, ridiculing myself for doing it, but excited nonetheless.

There was no visible person anywhere near my house, but, as I had surmised, there was a long piece of white paper hanging from my doorknob. I pulled it off and brought it inside, and then I tossed it right into the recycling bin, leaving the woman in the photo on it to smile up at the lid, offering her real estate services to no one.

"Jeez, Ella," I mumbled. Did I have to remind myself that I wasn't a character on a TV show? I took another look at my piece of posterboard, covered with names and connecting lines. I had planned on finding a space on the wall for it, but now that seemed like something only a crazy person would do. I decided to put it back in the closet instead.

Chapter 9: Questioning a Suspect

When I woke up in the morning, the Wilmette-Rutledge connection still seemed important, even if I was turning into some sort of obsessive crazy person, so I dug up the detective's card.

"Roth"

"Hello. This is Ella Graepenteck. I'm a witness in the Harvey Wil..."

"Yes! Hello!" He said it with such enthusiasm that it startled me. He seemed to be in a very good mood, or maybe he just really enjoyed his job. "What can I do for you, Ms. Graepenteck?"

"I think I may have some information for you, about the case."

"What kind of information?"

"Maybe a possible motive, to do with art."

"Art?"

"Yes, or maybe money connected to art, to a famous artist."

"Harvey Wilmette was connected to a famous artist?"

"Yes."

"Maybe you should come down to the station."

"Okay."

My mind wandered as I drove. I thought about Ezekiel Wilder, who left his big family and the farm in Nebraska to seek stardom in Hollywood, as so many people do. He got further than most. I wondered how he died. The brief obituary in the magazine said it was a respiratory infection. What did that mean, exactly? Maybe it was tuberculosis. Maybe he had lung cancer. Maybe it had nothing to do with his respiratory system at all. A gossip magazine might not be the most reliable source.

Thinking about death brought my thoughts back to Harvey Wilmette. What was he doing right before he died? Did he know he was in danger? Had someone threatened him? Maybe he thought he was just having a normal day at work, meeting with a potential customer, or a vendor, or someone more familiar. The detectives had asked me about his brother James. It was a horrible thought, but he wouldn't be the first man to have been killed by his brother.

Parking at the police station was easy, but walking through the gap in the wall and down the shadowy tunnel to the door was no less anxiety-inducing the second time.

There was a different young woman behind the front desk, her hair pulled back in the same kind of tight bun, but her hair was red, almost the same color as mine. I smiled at her, and she smiled back with that air of immediate familiarity that can arise when people have something unusual in common. Instead of just buzzing me through, she left a tall blond man at the desk and led me herself through the door and down the corridor to the second door. On the way I found out her name was Lesley and she had been a police officer for almost two years. The same remarkably hairless young man who had been at the inner door last time was there again. He opened it for me, and Lesley headed back to the front desk.

Detective Roth saw me through the glass wall, opened the glass door, and led me back to Detective Vasquez, sitting at his desk. I sat across from him, in the same rolling chair as the last time. After initial pleasantries I produced copies of the birth and census records that showed Harvey Wilmette was descended from Louis Wilmette, and explained Louis Wilmette's connection to F. H. Rutledge.

Detective Vasquez raised his eyebrows and pursed his lips as he perused the documents. At first he seemed impressed, but then he looked up and stared at me for a moment.

"What made you think to look for all this?"

"I'm a curious person, and a genealogist, and... It's also something I do for fun. It was a hobby before it was my business."

"What was the third thing?"

"What?"

"You are a curious person, and a genealogist, and... what? You were going to say a third thing."

I was afraid of how it would sound, but I couldn't think of a convincing lie, so I told the truth.

"I thought I recognized the name."

"What name? Wilmette?"

"Yes. I thought I had heard it before, and it was bothering me, so I looked him up."

"And did you? Hear it before?"

"Yes."

"You have an interest in twentieth century art?"

"No. Not exactly. Not in general."

Both detectives were staring at me now. They were beginning to make me nervous.

"My great grandmother probably knew them both,

Louis Wilmette and F. H. Rutledge. She was a student at the Chicago Art Institute at the same time they were."

Detective Vasquez leaned back in his chair.

"So you have a connection to the same artist."

"Yes."

"And didn't you also have a family connection to the guy you were looking up that day, the reason you were there when the body was discovered?"

"Well, the guy's friend, yes."

"The guy's friend."

There was a long moment while Detective Vasquez looked at me, bouncing slowly back and forth in his chair. It was unclear whether he was nodding at me or his head was moving up and down just because of the way the chair was moving. I couldn't see Detective Roth. He was now standing behind me, and it didn't seem like a good time to turn around. I felt a need to break the silence.

"It's strange, I know. I have no explanation. It's a ridiculous set of coincidences."

Detective Vasquez continued to stare and bounce, so I continued.

"I'm not a big fan of coincidences, in general, and I definitely don't like these. I really have no idea what is going on here."

I was startled, but then relieved, to hear Detective Roth's voice from behind me. He addressed me, but seemed to be aiming his voice at his colleague.

"And we were unaware of this connection until you brought it to us. You didn't have to tell us about it."

Detective Vasquez leaned forward and finally spoke, looking at Detective Roth, instead of at me.

"We probably would have discovered it eventually."

"Probably," said Roth, "but maybe not."

That seemed to annoy Vasquez, and he stood up, pointing to the papers on his desk, now looking at me again.

"Can we keep these things you brought?"

"Of course."

"Thank you for your assistance, Ms. Graepenteck. We may have more questions for you at a later time. You're not planning to travel any time soon, are you?"

"No."

"Good. Thank you again. You can go."

I stood up and headed out. Detective Roth came with me. I thought he would stop at the glass door, but he stayed right behind me, all the way across the room and into the corridor. He didn't speak, though, so finally I did.

"This situation really is bothering me, even keeping me up at night. I truly had nothing to do with any of it. I never heard of Harvey Wilmette until that day."

"I believe you."

I stopped walking and turned to look at him.

"Detective Vasquez doesn't seem to."

"It's not that he doesn't believe you. He hasn't decided yet. He's a good cop, an experienced detective. He's just thinking of all the angles."

"I hope he figures it out. I'm certainly having no luck trying."

"He will. He always does."

"What about you? Aren't you a good cop?"

"I'm learning."

I couldn't think of anything else to say. He was being very kind. Maybe he really believed me, or maybe this was some sort of good cop, bad cop technique. He could be pretending to be on my side so I would trust him enough to confess. I might actually have become a serious suspect in a murder investigation. This police detective, standing right in front of me, might think I was a murderer. He might be just waiting for the right moment to arrest me.

Suddenly the thing I wanted most in the world was to be out of that building and in my car. I was only a few steps from the door to that big front room, the one with the big front door, the way out. I conquered my instinct to run, and instead put out my hand to shake.

"Well, thank you, Detective Roth."

He shook my hand and said something I didn't hear clearly as I made my way through the door out of the hallway and closed it behind me. I waved to Lesley as I passed her but didn't break stride until I was outside and in the parking lot next to my little blue car. I realized I had been taking shallow breaths and consciously took a few deep ones. Maybe I had overreacted. Maybe I wasn't a suspect at all, or maybe I was, but Detective Roth was being nice to me because he didn't think I should be one. Maybe he felt sorry for me. Maybe he liked me.

That last thought sparked a happy feeling somewhere inside. I squelched it immediately.

"Idiot," I said to myself as I found my keys. I realized I had said it out loud, so I looked around. I saw no indication anyone had heard. Then, as if I needed an added bit of proof that I was indeed an idiot, I dropped my keys, and they went under the car. I was forced to get down on my hands and knees and reach past a crushed soda can and what looked like a wad of gum to retrieve them. Finally I was able to open the door and sit in the driver's seat. I took another deep breath and then strapped myself in for the drive home.

Traffic wasn't bad, but the minutes seemed like hours anyway.

Chapter 10: Back on Bluebird Avenue

I had been driving for about twenty of those very long minutes when my phone rang. It was Sara Markis. I pushed the button on the steering wheel.

"Hello, Sara."

"Hi! Oh wow, I'm so glad you picked up! I hate leaving voicemails, and then waiting for people to call back, and everything. Um, so, how are you?"

"I'm fine, thank you. What can I do for you?"

"I was wondering if maybe you might be able to stop by today, to talk about, you know, the research, and stuff. I have some questions about some things. Do you think you have time? It would be great if we could meet today, just for, like, an update, to make sure we're like, on the same page or whatever?"

"I don't see why not. I'm actually not far from you right now, if that works. Otherwise I could come later this afternoon."

"Yeah! Great! Um, just a sec."

She said something, but it was muffled. She was talking to someone, probably Andrew Cobb, the lawyer. Maybe she had her hand over the microphone. Then she came back and I heard her clearly.

"Sure, now works great!"

"I'm on my way."

Parking on Bluebird Avenue was no easier than before, but the walk from my car was just as pleasant. I strolled slowly, luxuriating in the filtered sunlight and the soft, faintly salty breeze. The front door to the building was unlocked, so I went in and continued my stroll up the stairs. Sara opened her apartment door before I had finished knocking on it. This time her T-shirt was pale pink and her nails were bright red, but otherwise she was dressed much the same as the last time, except that her hair was down, and she was wearing long, dangly, silver earrings. I was surprised to see that she seemed to be alone. Andrew, or whomever she had spoken to while we were on the phone, must have left.

"I'm so glad you could make it! Would you like some tea?"

"No thank you."

"Um, I'm going to have some anyway. I just really feel like tea for some reason. You don't mind, right?"

"Of course not."

"Come on in! Sit down! Relax!"

She gestured toward the sofa, so I sat there while she moved about in the kitchen.

I looked around the still excruciatingly white room. The shelves were occupied mostly by knickknacks, little figurines of cats and swans and girls in ball gowns, some glass, some ceramic, and there were quite a few photos in frames. One photo was of an older couple, probably Sara's parents. The rest were of groups of young people, mostly women, probably her friends. One seemed to have been taken at a ski resort. The others all looked like they were taken at restaurants, except for a few at the beach. There was one young man who appeared in several of the group photos, but rarely right next to Sara. He resembled her somewhat. A brother? A more distant relative? I didn't see any photos of Andrew Cobb. I couldn't imagine a scenario in which Sara had a boyfriend and did not have pictures of him on display, so that seemed an indication either that Cobb was not her boyfriend, or that my imagination was not up to the task at hand. Since criticism of my imagination has always centered around my having too much of it, never too little, the latter option seemed unlikely. Whatever there was between them must have been very new.

Finally she brought her tea in and sat down. I didn't see her phone, and wondered where it was. She must have had the same thought, because she got up again and went back to the kitchen. She came back with phone in hand, and laid it on the table next to her teacup.

"So, you have questions?"

"Yeah, well, um, first of all, how is the research going?"

"I've found it fairly easy to track the Wilder family back through census records. They came to Nebraska between 1860 and 1870. Before that they were in Indiana."

"Wow, it's amazing how you can find all that out." She was scrolling on her phone as she said it.

"There's so much online now. It's not all that difficult if you know how to look."

"Well I still think it's amazing, like truly amazing. I'm really super curious about that Edmund Walforth guy though. I can't believe I'm related to a moviestar!"

"Probably, although I really do recommend getting in touch with someone from the Wilder family and trying to get a DNA test. They're easy to do now. You might not be able to have the results in time for your grandmother's birthday, but I think it would be good to be sure."

She didn't put her phone down, but she did move her gaze from it to me. "Yeah, but I'm not sure how to get in touch with them, the Wilder family I mean, and it seems kind of awkward. I mean, what if they're super traditional? What if they don't know anything about my grandmother and don't want to know? It might be really uncomfortable, you know? The whole adoption thing."

"It could be."

"Yeah, and I'm just not sure I want to do that, you know? I mean, even if I do, I'm not sure how to go about it."

"Well, as I've said, that is not my area of expertise, but Isaac Wilder Jr. is, or at least was, a lawyer. Didn't that friend of yours who is a lawyer say he could help? Maybe he could contact him through his law firm. That way it wouldn't have to be so immediately personal."

"Andrew did say that, didn't he?"

She smiled wide, apparently at the thought of Andrew. She checked her phone again.

"Are you waiting for a call?"

"What? Oh. No. I mean, I don't mean to be rude or anything. It's just, you know, family stuff."

"Family stuff?"

"Oh! Not like genealogy family. My family, I mean, Markis family stuff. It's nothing. Just, like, some cousins coming into town or something. No big deal."

"Oh, I see."

"I am really curious about Edmund Walforth though. But it's so terrible what happened to that man at that office you went to. I still can't believe that. What was his name again?"

"Harvey Wilmette."

"Yeah, right, Harvey Wilmette. Do you know if they have found out yet what happened, I mean, who killed him and all that?"

"No. I don't know, but I don't think so."

"It's scary, actually knowing about a murder. It's weird, like being in the middle of a movie or something. It must be much worse for you. I mean, you actually saw the body, right?"

"Yes."

"I don't mean to be creepy or anything. I mean, I know it's a weird thing to ask, but I'm just curious, you know?"

"Curious about what, exactly?"

"Well, you know, what was it like?"

"Seeing the body?"

"Yeah."

"It was very strange. I don't know how to describe it."

"I'm sorry. You probably don't want to talk about it. I shouldn't have brought it up."

"No need to apologize, but you're right that I'm not particularly interested in discussing it."

"Sure. No problem."

"If you are interested in learning more about Edmund Walforth though, the man I was there to meet that day, Bob Ogilvie, has photos and magazine articles and documents from Walforth's work at California Pictures. I'm sure if you want those things, he'd still be happy to sell them to you."

"I think I would like that. It does seem maybe a little creepy, but I would kind of like to have some of those things. It would be great to be able to give my grandmother a photo of her birth father."

"I can put you in touch with Mr. Ogilvie." I considered asking for her phone, so I could put Ogilvie's contact info into it, or reading it out for her, so she could put it in herself, but she was so engrossed in tapping and scrolling that I didn't want to interrupt her. I got out my notepad and a pen instead. I looked him up on my phone and copied down all the pertinent information. She glanced at the piece of paper as I passed it across the table to her, then looked at her phone again. She tapped and scrolled. Then she looked up at me.

"Would I have to go to that office?"

"I doubt it. I'm sure he would come here, or meet you someplace else."

"That would be great."

"Did you have other questions? Do you want me to change the direction of my research? I'm focusing on tracing the Wilders back as far as I can."

"No, that's good. I'd like to know more about that. Where did you say they were before Nebraska?"

"Indiana."

"Yeah, I'd like to know more about that."

She kept scrolling on her phone. I waited for her to say something else, but she didn't.

"If there's nothing else, I'll head out and get back to work."

"Great, okay, thanks so much for coming!"

"You're welcome."

I reflected on our conversation as I drove away. There was something about it I didn't like, but I wasn't sure exactly what. She had seemed a bit nervous, but there could be any number of explanations for that. We could have accomplished the same thing easily over the phone, but some people just prefer to meet in person. She wasn't the first client to have wasted some of my time. I didn't particularly like her, but she wasn't unique in that respect either. In any case, I was going to work through the hours she'd paid for as soon as possible, and if she wanted to buy more I would say I was too busy. Maybe it was the fact that I had seen a dead body while working for her, or maybe something else was making me uneasy, but I decided was going to end this association as quickly as I could.

Chapter 11: Going Home

It occurred to me that I was hungry, and just after I had that thought, I saw the sign for Norm's on Pico. Perfect. I was in the exact right mood for a club sandwich. It was early for lunch, so it was easy to park and there were plenty of empty tables. I ordered and got my Kindle out of my bag. I never go anywhere without something to read. You never know when you're going to be stuck in a line or waiting for someone who's late.

I looked through my long list of titles for just the right one to suit my current state of mind and stopped at P. G. Wodehouse. That was it. I clicked on <u>Right Ho, Jeeves</u> and was happier within minutes. By the time my sandwich arrived I already felt significantly less stressed. I started to believe that everything would turn out fine.

Still, I didn't feel like going straight home, and I hadn't been to the beach in a while, so when I finished eating I drove out to the Santa Monica pier. The sound of the ocean somehow always eases the tension in my neck. I kept my shoes on until I crossed the hot sand, but when I got near the water I took them off and rolled my pants up to my knees. I carried my shoes and meandered along the edges of the breaking waves, watching my feet make prints in the wet sand, occasionally letting the cold water splash around my ankles.

My favorite time at the beach is early morning, when it's quiet and there aren't many people around, but it's nice even in the tourist spattered afternoons. That day, like most days, people who had come from far away were excited to be there. A group of kids chased seagulls. A toddler cried when she found out how cold the water was, and as her mother rushed to comfort her, all the other adults nearby smiled in sympathy. These exact same scenarios play out every day, with different people. It was all very predictable, and predictability can be boring, but only when you've had too much of it. When you're feeling frazzled, boring is beautiful.

After about fifteen minutes and a frisbee that narrowly missed my head, it started to seem less beautiful, so I turned around and headed back to my car. It didn't bother me to get a little sand in it. I drove home, locked the car and the garage, and started along the paving stone path toward my back door.

Then I stopped. Something didn't look quite right. Was the door not completely closed? I scanned the back of the house. One of the windows was broken. In my head I yelled at myself the way I often yell at the television when characters find themselves in this kind of situation. "Don't go in there, you idiot! Stay outside and call the police!" Unfortunately, as my mother, many teachers, a few employers, and a couple of ex-boyfriends would confirm, I frequently just won't listen.

I pushed at the door. It opened easily, but the lock didn't seem broken. Whoever had come in had probably gone through the broken window and come out this way, in such a rush that they didn't check to make sure the door was closed. It was possible, though, that someone was still in there. Well aware of how stupid I was being, I stepped inside.

Aside from the broken glass on the floor, the kitchen seemed undisturbed. The living room and dining area seemed fine too. The second bedroom/office was a different story. Drawers were open. File folders and papers were everywhere. I was glad I had been carrying my laptop with me, and that I don't keep a desktop computer. There was some destruction in the bedroom too.

Nothing obvious seemed to be missing. All my jewelry, none of which was particularly valuable, was there. I didn't have any drugs, except over the counter ones, but the bathroom didn't seem to have been touched, so they weren't after that. They had ransacked the closets, which I thought was odd. It seemed like they were looking for information. Do people keep important information in their closets? Maybe some do. In any case, the would-be thieves had made a substantial mess. It would take a while to determine if anything was missing from my files.

Finally, I got around to doing the smart thing. I called Detective Roth.

"Roth."

"Hello, this is Ella Graepenteck. Someone broke into my house."

"Are you there now?"

"Yes. Whoever it was is gone."

"Don't touch anything. Did you call 911?"

"No, just you."

"I'll send someone over to take a report, but I'm also going to come take a look."

He arrived about ten minutes after the local officers. I showed him, as I had shown them, all the places that had been disturbed.

"What kind of information do you keep in those files?"

"All my personal records, financial, medical, everything, and all my business information."

"Personal information about your clients?"

"Yes, anything that is pertinent to my research."

"We will need to figure out what they took, if anything, as quickly as possible. This might be totally unrelated to the murder case, but I'd be surprised. You know, your information about the art connection was helpful. It turns out Wilmette was involved in some illegal art deals."

"Really?"

"Someone might think you have information about him or about the art."

"I don't, though. At least I don't think I do."

"They think you do."

He looked down at his notepad, wrote something.

"Is there... Do you have someone you can stay with for a while? It may not be safe here. They might come back."

"It seems like they searched pretty thoroughly, so if they didn't find what they wanted, there's no reason for them to come back."

"They might not see it that way."

"I could stay with my mother. She has plenty of room, and a state of the art security system."

"Good. As soon as we're done here you can pack some things."

"Okay."

He looked at his notepad again.

"Can you give me that address? Your mother's."

He wrote it down, and then he stared at what he had written. Without looking up, he asked, "and your mother's name?"

"Patricia Graepenteck."

He wrote that down too, but hesitatingly. I could see the next question forming in his head, and I decided to save him some time.

"Patricia de Brisay Graepenteck."

At that he looked up.

"You recognized the address?"

He didn't answer.

"It was on some sort of list of de Brisay properties? That property, though, turned out not to be connected to whatever it was you were investigating, right?"

He still didn't answer.

"Right?"

"Yes. Right."

"What were you investigating, anyway? Never mind. You can't tell me. I know. Look, there are a lot of de Brisays in Los Angeles, and yes, I am probably related to whomever you were investigating, but only distantly, and my mother and that house have nothing to do with whatever crime you were solving."

"Okay."

"Whether you believe me or not, it's the truth."

"What's important is that it will be a safe place for you to stay."

"It will."

"Good."

The suspicious look that lurked in his eyes when we first met was back, but I didn't think further explanation from me at that moment would send it away, so I didn't try. Instead I focused on what I had to do next.

I decided it would frighten my mother less if I just showed up, clearly safe and able to explain everything in person, than it would if I called first and told her why I was coming. I texted her that I would be dropping by after I got some work done.

That evening I put a suitcase full of things the police let me take from my house into my car, and then I drove to Laurel Canyon and up the narrow curves to the top of Alta Brea Crescent. As I walked through the front door my mother walked out of the kitchen.

"To what do I owe this delightful surprise?"

"Well, you're not going to like the answer to that."

Her smile dropped and she sat down on the nearest chair.

"It's okay, Mom, everything is fine. I'm fine. Nothing serious happened."

"What happened?"

"Someone broke into my house."

"What!"

"There's no damage except a broken window, and as far as I can tell they didn't take anything."

"Then why did they break in?"

"Maybe to look for something in my files."

"What!"

"It's probably nothing."

"You're not going back there. You're staying here. Did you call the police?"

"Yes. I called those detectives, the ones investigating that thing in Hollywood."

"That murder, you mean. For heaven's sake, Ella."

"I know. It's crazy."

"You are definitely not going back there."

"No, I'm not. The detective actually said I shouldn't. That's why I'm here."

"Good! Well, that detective has some brains, anyway. Did you bring anything?"

"I have a bag in the car."

"Well bring it in!"

I brought in my suitcase and took it up to my old room. It was a guest room now, with pale blue walls and white curtains. The bedspread was white with sprays of yellow flowers. I felt like I was in a quiet little bed and breakfast. It wasn't my childhood room anymore, but it was almost as comforting as if it were. I hadn't realized how rattled I had been by the break-in until I walked through the door to that room and noticed how safe I felt there. I put my suitcase down on the floor, walked over to the bed, sat on it, and stared out the window at the familiar view.

Chapter 12: The Landridge Family

I woke up feeling disoriented. It took me a moment to remember where I was, and why. When I did, I put a sweatshirt on over the T-shirt and sweatpants I had slept in and went down to the kitchen. My mother was there, drinking coffee.

"Good morning!"

"Good morning."

"There are fresh eggs, and fresh bread, and orange juice."

"Thanks. I think I'll start with a glass of water."

I took a glass from a cabinet and filled it from the faucet dedicated to filtered drinking water.

"How are you feeling this morning?"

"I'm not sure. Two weeks ago I had never, ever been among the first at the scene of a crime, and now I'm averaging one a week. I don't know how to process that. I'm flabbergasted."

"Understandably."

"Who'd have thought genealogy could be such a dangerous profession? I've never had any involvement with crime before."

"I know."

"I've gotten one speeding ticket in my life, on San Vicente Boulevard, on that long, empty, straight stretch by the golf course, and who hasn't driven too fast there?"

"No one."

"I suppose I got a lot of parking tickets when I lived in Boston, but come on! There's no place to park in Boston."

"Very true."

"I do remember being the victim of a crime once."

"When was that?"

"I had my pocket picked in New York."

"Oh, yes. I remember that."

"But only once. All the time I spent there, and only once, and never anything worse. I have been there so many times. New York City! Sometimes in very questionable neighborhoods, and never, ever was I mugged or assaulted or anything violent."

"It's quite a good record."

"Now here I am, in my hometown, and without warning, for no reason, I happened to come across a murdered person, and a week later my house gets burgled. What's going to happen next Monday?"

"Let's hope nothing."

"Is anyone coming to the house today?"

"No. Gardeners on Mondays. Maids on Thursdays. Nothing special scheduled for today. It should be quiet."

"Good."

I spent a lot of the day reading and watching old movies and lying on my old bed staring at the ceiling. Every few hours I went down to the kitchen to get something to eat, but other than that, I barely left my bedroom. After breakfast, my mother was out all day, running errands and meeting friends and getting things done, so I had the whole house to myself, but still I stayed in that room.

Around 3:00 p.m. I decided I needed to go somewhere else, if only downstairs, so I took my laptop and went down to the family room. I went down the main staircase and then walked along it toward the kitchen, until I reached the small door tucked under the stairs. It looked like the kind of door that would be locked, but it never was.

I opened it. Walking into that room was like entering a cave, but only because the drapes were all closed.

I felt for a switch on the wall, flipped it, and the drapes all simultaneously and slowly drew themselves, revealing floor to ceiling windows that took up most of the semicircular wall around the room. From any point in that room you can see the intricately arranged garden of native Californian plants, with pathways of finely ground gravel winding around and through it. The garden continues far down the hill, until it runs into the impenetrable hedge of trees and bushes concealing the array of walls and fences, some electrified, that surround the property. A sense of gratitude to my ancestors for granting me access to such a peaceful, protected haven was briefly disturbed by thoughts about the crooked ways they may have obtained the money to do so, but the gratitude beat back the guilt.

I opened up my laptop and indulged in my hobby of looking for genealogical information about people related to me, and people connected with them, and people who weren't connected with them, if they were interesting. It occurred to me to look up Emily Dickinson. Maybe my isolation in the house made me think of her. I didn't know anything about her family. Maybe it would be interesting. It amused me for a while, but nothing seemed able to keep me from ruminating on everything that had happened over the last couple of weeks. How did I get into this situation? Who killed Harvey Wilmette, and why, and what did it have to do with me? I couldn't stop the thoughts from coming, so I stopped trying.

I decided to look at all the information I had on my computer about Violet and Harriet Eylerbetz and their brothers and that circle of artists in Chicago in the early 1900s. There had to be some kind of clue there. Over the years I had saved census records, vital records, lists of students at the Chicago Art Institute, newspaper articles from the time, and random documents I didn't remember saving. I pored over everything, to refresh my memory and to see if I could discover anything new.

Violet's circle of friends included her brothers Frederick and Ulysses (not a particularly unusual name at the time) and fellow art students F. H. Rutledge, Louis A. Wilmette, and a man called Elbert J. Landridge. Landridge had two sisters, Rosemary and Matilda, who were not students at the Art Institute, but who were mentioned in a few newspaper articles. Louis Wilmette had a cousin, Margaret Wilmette, who was a student at the Institute and apparently good friends with Violet. So there was a closer connection than I had remembered between the Wilmette family and mine. Harriet, when she was in Chicago, was also part of the group.

So, there were five young men and up to five young women in the group. All of the men and two of the women were art students. Rutledge was the only one who became world famous, but both Eylerbetz brothers and Louis Wilmette went on to make their livings from art. I was curious about Elbert Landridge. I had forgotten all about him, and I never knew much. This seemed like a good time to learn more.

Knowing the names of his sisters, it was not hard to find his family in the 1900 census. A search pulled up several Landridge families in Chicago, including one with a son named Albert and one with a son named Ellert. They both had sisters, but Albert's were named Helen, Anne, and Marjorie. Ellert's were Rosemary and Matilda. That settled that. Ellert was Elbert.

These Landridges appeared to be quite wealthy. Their household listed ten live-in servants, including a butler, a cook, a chauffeur, maids, and gardeners. The head of household was Elbert's older brother Herbert Landridge Jr., who was listed as 28 years old and recently married to a woman named Elizabeth, who was 22. His occupation was listed as capitalist, which sounds odd now, but it was not an unusual designation for wealthy men in the 1900 census. Landridge's mother, Eleanor, was widowed. Rosemary was listed as 22 and Matilda as 21, but experience told me they were probably older than that. I have seen many people appear to age only a few years over the ten year gap between censuses. This tends to be especially true of unmarried women, but I have also found plenty of married men claiming to be a good ten to fifteen years younger than they are. That's why, when estimating age, I always try to find a person on the earliest census possible. It's not unusual for someone to be listed as, for example, 2 in 1850 and 12 in 1860, but 18 in 1870 and 24 in 1880. On this particular census page, from 1900, Elbert was listed as age 20, occupation student. He seemed to be the youngest child in the family.

Since the 1890 U.S. census was almost entirely destroyed by fire, in most cases the next one back in time from 1900 is the one from 1880, so that was the next place I looked. I found the Landridge family in Chicago, in the same house, with Herbert Sr. still alive. Elbert was listed as just three months old, so he probably actually was 20 in 1900. His brother Herbert was listed as 8 years old, which corroborated his being 28 in 1900, but his sisters were 5 and 3, not 2 and 1. It seemed clear each had shaved a few years off her age in 1900. I didn't judge. It was none of my business how old Rosemary and Matilda wanted people to think they were.

So, in 1903, when he started attending the Chicago Art Institute, Elbert was probably living in his fancy family house, with his mother and brother and sisters and lots of servants. His brother seemed to be providing for the family, likely assisted by an inheritance from his father, which left Elbert free to go to art school.

The next step was to move ahead in time. I looked at the 1910 census. By then, Violet and Harriet were both married and living in L.A. Frederick and Ulysses and their mother had joined their brother Edward Jr. in New York. F. H. Rutledge was already making a name for himself as an artist, still living in Chicago. I found both him and Louis Wilmette there in the 1910 census, both single, each living alone, quite near each other, both listed with the occupation of artist.

Elbert Landridge was still in the same house, with his brother and his mother. His sisters were no longer there. Presumably they had gotten married. Herbert Jr. and his wife Elizabeth now had two children, Herbert III and Eleanor, and Elbert was married to a woman named Mary. I searched for marriage records and found the right one. It listed Elbert as Albert, but it had to be them. Albert Landridge, age 29, parents Herbert and Eleanor, married Mary Millbrook in 1909. In 1910, Elbert's occupation was listed as artist.

I knew F. H. Rutledge spent most of World War I in Europe, where he married a French woman, and then they moved to New York. Sure enough, in 1920, there they were, with their two young sons, one of whom would die in a few years. The other would die in World War II before having the chance to get married or have children. That would be the sad end of any direct heirs. Louis Wilmette was living in Los Angeles in 1920, and recently married, with his occupation still listed as artist, but he was an employee of California Pictures. Perhaps he painted scenery, or portraits of stars.

Elbert Landridge's situation had changed somewhat, although he was still in the same house in Chicago, with his brother. His mother wasn't listed. A search for death records confirmed that she had died in 1913. Herbert Jr. and Elizabeth still seemed the same. He was listed as a manufacturer, and their children were now teenagers. Elbert and Mary now had a son named John. Elbert's occupation, though, was no longer anything to do with art. He was a manufacturer like his brother. That could have been because he wasn't successful as an artist, or because he was needed in the business, or both.

By 1930 little had changed for Rutledge or Wilmette, except that Louis Wilmette Jr. had been born. The only changes for the Landridge family were that Herbert Jr.'s daughter Eleanor, who had probably gotten married, was no longer living there, and that the number of servants had been reduced to two. Cutting ten servants down to two seemed significant. Perhaps the crash of 1929 had some impact on the family income.

1940 is the last year for which federal census records are publicly available. They were released by the National Archives in 2012, and the 1950 census records will be released in 2022, because of what is known as the 72-Year Rule. This rule has been in force since the 1950s, and was the result of much debate about the protection of personal information and when it should be made available for research purposes. Presumably the number 72 had something to do with average lifespans at the time. If that is the case, it may be time to update the rule. Many people who appear on the 1950 census will still be alive in 2022. An extension of the time would not be helpful to genealogists, however, so I have mixed feelings on the matter.

As the 1940 census records were in fact released after 72 years, I could see that by 1940, F. H. Rutledge, now a widower, was living on the ranch he bought in his home state of South Dakota, enjoying the life of an established, famous artist. Louis A. Wilmette was living with his wife and teenage son in L.A., still working for California Pictures. They had a live-in maid.

An entirely different family was living in what had been the Landridge house in Chicago. Herbert Jr. was now dead. Elbert was a head of household living in an apartment. His occupation was listed as manager. His son John and his nephew Herbert were both living with him and working as clerks. His wife Mary and his widowed sister-in-law Elizabeth seemed to be in charge of running the household. There were no live-in servants. Clearly the

Depression had not been good to the Landridge family. Maybe they harbored resentment. Maybe Elbert would have come to friends who had fared better for help. Maybe he had descendants who were still bitter. Maybe somewhere in those events there was a motive for murder.

Chapter 13: A Round Table Meeting

The history of the Landridge family occupied me until I fell asleep Tuesday night. I woke up early enough on Wednesday to have breakfast with my mother, after her morning walk and before her preparations for whatever activities she had in store that day.

"I don't want to push you, but don't you think you ought to leave the house today?"

"I left the house yesterday."

"You did? Where did you go?"

"I took a walk. I went all the way down to the hedge."

"Very funny. I know you have this need to hibernate sometimes, but I worry about you."

"I know, and I appreciate it. I'm doing some online research today, but I might go out. If not today, then definitely tomorrow."

"Okay."

I went back upstairs and on to my computer for more genealogy research. About 9:30 in the morning I got a call from the police station.

"Hello?"

"Hello Ms. Graepenteck. This is Detective Roth."

"Hello Detective Roth."

"Ms. Graepenteck, could you come to the station this afternoon, about two o'clock?"

"I think so. Is there news about the break-in at my house?"

"Possibly. We did find a couple of partial footprints outside your broken window. We can fill you in further when you come in."

"Okay, then I'll be there at two o'clock."

"Good."

He was very businesslike, not displaying any of the kind concern he had shown the day of the break-in. That could be because Detective Vasquez was in the room, or because the kind concern was just an act, or for any number of other reasons. I told myself to stop thinking about it, but I didn't stop, and before I knew it a couple of hours had passed.

I made myself a sandwich for lunch, and continued to watch the clock. I wondered if a couple of partial footprints would be enough evidence to catch whoever broke into my house. I wondered if there might be descendants of Elbert Landridge in L.A., and what specific motives they might have to kill Harvey Wilmette, and what any of it could possibly have to do with me. Finally it got to be one o'clock.

I gathered up my notes on the Landridge family and put them and my laptop into my computer bag. Then I looked in the mirror. I tried to tell myself this was business. I was helping with a murder investigation. It didn't matter how I looked. But myself told me the hell with it, I'm putting on makeup and earrings and a blue shirt that brings out my eyes.

My ruminations continued on the now familiar drive to the police station. The tunnel-like entrance was slightly less intimidating this time, because I knew just what to expect on the other side of the door. Lesley, the redhead, was behind the front desk. I smiled at her, and she smiled back, but I thought I detected some unease. Her smile was a little stiff, her shoulders a little tense. Maybe some investigation unrelated to me was making her nervous.

Maybe I was the one who was nervous, and the tenseness I detected was all in my imagination.

Lesley let me in the door to the back, but didn't accompany me down the hall this time. The same young man who was there the last time let me into the big room with the glass wall. Detective Roth saw me from behind it and opened the glass door for me.

"Thank you for coming. We're all in here."

He guided me to a sort of conference room. I thought it was strange that he used the word "all" to refer to just him and Detective Vasquez, but when I got inside the room I understood. There were five people in there.

Detective Vasquez was sitting at the far side of a round table. To his left sat Barbara Milvander, wearing a shiny, bright green blouse and large stud earrings shaped like golden knots, but no scarves this time. To her left sat Bob Ogilvie, in what might have been his only blue suit. To the detective's right sat another woman and to her right another man. I had never seen either of them before, but I was fairly confident that they had to be Miranda and James Wilmette. She had long, straight, black hair parted in the middle, and thick mascara emphasizing very large, dark eyes. She was wearing something simple and black with a

120

square neckline. Her husband was just as thin and just as bald as Harvey had been. What hair he had was grey, and he was wearing a grey suit. Even his eyes were grey. It almost looked as if their side of the table was in black and white, and the other side in color.

All faces turned toward me as I entered the room. No one looked happy, and everyone except Detective Vasquez looked nervous. I wasn't here because they'd found a few footprints. This was clearly some sort of gathering of suspects in the murder of Harvey Wilmette. That made me one of them.

There were two empty chairs left at the table. I sat next to Bob Ogilvie, and Detective Roth sat between me and James Wilmette. Detective Vasquez made introductions, and he seemed to be watching all of us carefully. I saw nothing noteworthy about any of our reactions, except that we all seemed anxious. Detective Vasquez started talking about Harvey.

"Mr. Wilmette made a will about ten years ago, and we have found no indication of any later wills. Are any of you aware of any new will he might have made since then?"

Everyone looked around at everyone else questioningly. The answer to the detective's question seemed to be no.

"Are any of you aware of the contents of the will he made ten years ago?"

Bob shifted in his chair. James cleared his throat. Miranda looked at James, but Bob was the first to speak.

"Oh, well, um, Harvey and I both, at that time, about ten years ago, we made wills. Um, it should, I haven't seen it, myself, but I think it should say that his half of the business... Well, we both put in our wills, then, that we made, at the same time, we said we would leave each other our half, I mean, of the business."

Miranda blurted, "Is that true? Detective?"

"Is that not what you expected, Mrs. Wilmette?"

James answered before Miranda could.

"I believe that is correct. It is my understanding, not having actually seen the will, but from conversations with my brother before..." He cleared his throat again, and Miranda placed her hand on his arm. "Before his tragic passing, my brother indicated to me that his half of the business he shared with Mr. Ogilvie would go to him, and the rest, his share of our family inheritance, which is essentially all there would be, as I understand it, would go to me."

"Yes, that's right." Miranda flushed, but she was recovering herself, and she smiled gently as she spoke. "I remember now. You explained it to me, Jimmy. I had forgotten." She released an apologetic little laugh and glanced anxiously at Detective Vasquez, who seemed to be enjoying directing this show.

"You are correct," he announced. "Mr. Wilmette's lawyer will be sending you copies of the will, and you will see that is exactly what it says. Mr. Ogilvie gets the business and Mr. Wilmette gets everything else."

"Such as it is," said James. "There isn't much. I think the business must be worth more." Miranda nodded along with his words.

"Oh, now, what does that mean?" Bob sat up a little straighter, and I could see sweat dripping from his forehead and getting caught in his eyebrows. "The business isn't much either, definitely not enough to kill for, if that's what you're trying to say."

Some incoherent bluster ensued, and Detective Vasquez put a quick stop to it, but I didn't pay much attention to the details, because I was looking at Barbara.

Her eyes were red, and despite what looked like great effort on her part to keep tears from forming, her cheeks were wet, and there were some small dark spots on her bright green blouse, where drops had fallen. If I had been sitting next to her, I would have handed her the pack of tissues I had in my purse, but it seemed too awkward to try to reach around Bob. I was about to get up and walk around him when Detective Vasquez addressed her directly.

"Ms. Milvander, did you and Mr. Wilmette ever discuss his will?"

She shook her head slowly, but kept looking down at the table.

"What about his life insurance policy?"

Four heads turned simultaneously toward Detective Vasquez. Actually, it must have been five heads, including mine. Detective Roth must have known that was coming. He kept looking at all the rest of us.

Barbara shook her head again, but this time she also spoke, sniffling and wiping her eyes as she did so.

"We never talked about anything like that. We didn't talk about the future much. Harvey liked to, you know, live in the moment."

"So you were unaware, Ms. Milvander, that four years ago Mr. Wilmette took out a life insurance policy and named you as the beneficiary?"

"What? Me? No!" A fresh wave of tears started to fall. "I mean, yes, I was unaware. Really? He named me?"

"He never discussed it with you?"

She was shaking her head rapidly now, so much so that some tendrils of her heavily sprayed cloud of hair moved from their carefully arranged positions. "No. Never. Not ever."

"Well, he did have a life insurance policy. He took it out four years ago, and named you as the sole beneficiary, and he kept up the payments. The last one was three days before he died."

I could see a question in the eyes of James and Miranda, the same question trying to get out of both of them. Miranda was the less restrained, so it came out of her mouth.

"How much was it for? The insurance policy. How much?"

Detective Vasquez paused for a moment, apparently for effect, looked directly at Barbara, and said, "two million dollars."

Chapter 14: Some Genealogical Research

Several things happened simultaneously. James and Miranda both gasped, and Miranda tightened her grasp on James' arm, digging her fingernails into it, but he didn't seem to notice. Bob said something that sounded like "Oho!" and patted Barbara's hand. They all stared at Barbara. She stared at Detective Vasquez for a moment, her eyes perfect weepy circles and her mouth a capital "O", and then she launched a fresh, even larger wave of tears, this time accompanied by loud sobs and shaking shoulders. Bob patted one of those shoulders the best he could, with all the shaking, and I finally did get up and bring her that pack of tissues.

I went back to my seat and took another look around. Barbara couldn't stop sobbing. Bob was focused on feeble attempts to soothe her. James and Miranda continued to stare at Barbara, but the initial shock seemed to be wearing off. Miranda had moved her hand from James' arm, and he was rubbing the place where her fingernails had been. Both detectives kept moving their gaze around the table, examining all of our reactions.

James raised his voice, to be heard over Barbara's sobs. "So, Detective, is this what you brought us here for? This melodrama?"

"I brought you here, Mr. Wilmette, to make sure you all knew the financial ramifications of your brother's unfortunate death."

"You mean who benefits from his death, who had a financial motive to kill him. What about her?" He pointed to me. "She's not in his will, or his insurance policy. He didn't even know her. Why is she here?"

Detective Vasquez stood up, smiling the resigned smile of the nearly exasperated parent. "Mr. Wilmette, you know I can't answer that kind of question."

James made a sound that was half a laugh and half a grunt. "Next you're going to say, 'I ask the questions around here!' It's like some stupid movie. What is all this? It's ridiculous! Are you charging any of us with anything?"

Rather than answering the question, the detective just calmly said, "We appreciate your coming in, and you and your wife are free to leave. You are all free to leave, although we may need to bring you in for more questions at a later date."

James and Miranda made a show of leaving in a huff. Bob helped a still weepy Barbara out of the room. I stayed exactly where I was, sitting in my seat. Detective Vasquez was looking at me. Detective Roth may have been looking at me too, but I couldn't tell, because he was sitting right next to me, and I was looking across the table at Detective Vasquez.

"Why AM I here?"

Detective Vasquez didn't answer. He just continued to look at me.

"Because I'm a suspect?"

He kept looking at me, but he sat down.

"But I don't benefit from his death."

"Not in any way we have found."

I turned to Detective Roth.

"Didn't you say something about footprints found outside my window?"

I seemed to have startled him a little, but he recovered quickly.

"Yes, we found two partial footprints, so when we have a suspect, we have some evidence to match."

"But you don't have a suspect."

"No. Not yet."

"Well, even if you do think I might be a murderer, you may be interested in some information I have come across."

Both detectives looked at me expectantly.

"There was another family that was connected to the Wilmettes and F. H. Rutledge and my great grandmother's family. The Landridges. I've tracked them up to 1940. They were still living in Chicago then, but the Wilmettes were already in L.A., and the Landridges probably knew that."

"Why does that matter?" asked Detective Vasquez.

"Elbert Landridge was an art student at the Chicago Art Institute, at the same time as F. H. Rutledge and Louis Wilmette and my great grandmother. They all knew each other. They were a circle of friends, along with Wilmette's cousin and Landridge's sisters."

The expression on the detective's face remained skeptical.

"The Landridges were a wealthy family, very wealthy, lots of servants, until around 1930."

Detective Roth spoke. "They lost it in the Depression?"

"It looks that way. Meanwhile, F. H. Rutledge was a big success, a famous artist, and Louis Wilmette had already been in Los Angeles for a while, working for California Pictures."

Roth grew more enthusiastically interested. "The same place Edmund Walforth and Reginald Ellis worked."

"Exactly. I haven't been able to pinpoint why all this matters, but it seems like too many coincidences."

The balance of suspicion and curiosity in Detective Vasquez' face began shifting toward the latter, but he didn't speak. Detective Roth continued, though.

"Elbert Landridge was not a successful artist?"

"No. He went to work in the family business, which apparently didn't go very well. Meanwhile, the Eylerbetz boys were making their living as portrait artists in New York, Wilmette had some sort of artistic function in the movies, and Rutledge was famous. Landridge was the only man in their group who had no art-related success at all."

"So maybe he was bitter." Roth was sounding more and more enthusiastic about this line of inquiry.

Detective Vasquez joined in, and the two detectives started talking to each other, as if I wasn't there.

"Maybe he asked for help and didn't get it."

"Or maybe he did get it and was resentful."

While they continued to debate the possibilities, I opened my computer bag and pulled out my laptop. Finally I interrupted them by saying, "Can I get on the wifi here?"

The detectives looked at me. Detective Vasquez asked, "Why?"

"Those guys you're talking about are all dead. Harvey Wilmette was Louis' grandson. Maybe Elbert Landridge had a grandson too, or a granddaughter. I might be able to find out right now, if I can get online."

Detective Roth looked at Detective Vasquez, who nodded, and then Roth turned to me.

"You can use my computer."

I put my laptop back in my bag, and we all got up and left the conference room.

I stood away from the desk to give Detective Roth privacy while he signed on to his computer and went through whatever protocols he needed to go through to get an internet connection and an open browser, and then he got up from his chair and gestured to me to replace him there. I sat down, and both detectives hovered behind me.

I logged into my favorite genealogy website and started looking up Landridges. I started by looking for John

Landridge, son of Elbert and Mary. Within a few minutes I had found a California Death Index record that looked like a possibility.

"This looks good," I said, and the detectives leaned closer. "It's a death record for a man named John Landridge, whose mother's maiden name was Millbrook. That was Elbert's wife Mary's maiden name. This John Landridge died in 1991."

Detective Vasquez peered at the screen. "In Los Angeles County?"

"Yes, but it might not be the same guy. Here's a Social Security Death Index record. Let's take a look at that." I clicked on it. "So here's the John Landridge who died in Los Angeles County on September 20th, 1991, and it says he obtained his social security number in Illinois. So this John Landridge was born in 1917, which is about when our John Landridge was born, and his mother's maiden name was Millbrook, and he moved from Illinois to Los Angeles. It's not definitive proof, but it looks like this is the same man."

"But he died in 1991."

"Maybe he had kids. Let's see what else we can find out about him."

I looked through Los Angeles city directories, and the only John Landridge I could find had a wife named Helen. They were listed as early as 1950. I found a listing on a marriage index for John Landridge and Helen Hale in Los Angeles in 1949.

Detective Vasquez seemed impressed. "All these records are just right there, online?"

"More and more every day. Let's look for birth records for Landridges in Los Angeles."

Four came up. I clicked on them one at a time. Alexander Landridge's mother's maiden name was Robertson, and he was born in 1946. Beatrice was born in 1952, but her mother's maiden name was Sanchez. Joseph seemed likely to be Alexander's brother. His mother's maiden name was Robertson too. The last one was Lucinda.

"There it is, fellas."

Roth read out the information. "Born 1951 in Los Angeles, mother's maiden name Hale. Lucinda Landridge. Sounds like a moviestar."

"Maybe it was intended to."

After several minutes fruitlessly looking for more about Lucinda Landridge, I decided there was a better way.

"Detectives, I don't think I'm going to find what we're looking for online, but I know where I can find more. I can go there tomorrow. The good news is I didn't find any death record for her, which doesn't necessarily mean she's still alive, but she might be."

Detective Vasquez leaned on the back of the chair, making it creak and making me hope it was stronger than he was. "So let me just make sure I've got this straight. All these people were in Los Angeles at the same time, Louis Wilmette Jr. and John Landridge, and your great grandmother."

"And her sister, who was Reginald Ellis' mother, and whose husband was an executive at California Pictures."

"You're right. Definitely too many coincidences, but still no clear motive. So Harvey Wilmette was Louis Wilmette's grandson."

"And Lucinda Landridge was Elbert Landridge's granddaughter."

"And your mother? or was it your father?"

"My father was Violet Eylerbetz's grandson."

"And Louis Wilmette was the heir of F. H. Rutledge."

"Yes."

"So maybe Harvey Wilmette had something that Lucinda Landridge or someone in her family wanted."

"Maybe."

"So where is this you're going tomorrow?"

"The County Registrar/Recorder. There are still a lot of records that aren't online."

"So you'll call us if you find anything." It was a statement, not a question.

"Of course."

Detective Roth walked me out. We passed that same young officer in the hallway.

"So that's what being a genealogist is like?"

"Some of the time. It's not always that easy. I actually like it better when it's not that easy."

"What do you mean?"

"I like solving puzzles. For example, I love searching census records. There are so many misspellings and wrong names and incorrect ages and places of birth. People who haven't seen them don't realize that those old census records were all handwritten, and the information didn't always come from the people themselves. It might have come from neighbors, or the people themselves might have lied. You have to decipher handwriting, and a lot of the indexing is really bad. I'm grateful to the people who enter all those names into searchable indexes, but they sometimes come up with the craziest interpretations of words and letters. Depending on the database and the index and the algorithms of the search functions, you have to try all kinds of different combinations. You can find some things by what names sound like, but more often it's about what they look like. I once found a Helmut Schneider, spelled perfectly correctly on the actual record, listed in the index as Habnol Sdmaicler."

"I get it. Puzzles."

I expected him to leave me at the door to the main lobby, but he kept walking with me. I smiled and waved to Lesley as we passed through the room.

"And then there's putting together lots of pieces of information to form a picture. Say there are six men with the same name, born around the same time, and you are looking for an exact birthdate. You need to find some other way of differentiating them, say by parents' names. Maybe the birthdate record doesn't have parents' names but it has addresses. Then if you can find something else that has both parents' names and addresses, you can find the right birthdate through the address."

136

"It sounds a lot like detective work."

"Does it? But in my work, everyone involved is dead, except the clients."

"Sort of the opposite of mine."

"I guess so."

The setting sun hit me right in the eyes as we emerged from the building. It was later than I thought. That sun was going to be annoying as I drove home. I headed toward my car, and the detective kept walking with me.

"What about your client?"

"What about her?"

"She is related to the actor who worked for California Pictures."

"Almost definitely."

"She showed you a birth certificate?"

"A copy of one, yes."

"Do you have proof that she is who she says she is?"

"No. She told me her grandmother was adopted and showed me the copy of the birth certificate and that's about it."

"Maybe she's part of the Landridge family."

"It's possible. I've been vaguely suspicious of her for a while, but I haven't been able to figure out exactly why. I

137

should be able to find out tomorrow if she is connected to the Landridges."

I was very aware of his closeness to me as I unlocked the car and opened the door.

"So you'll call us with what you find?" This time it sounded like a question.

"Yes."

"I guess I'll talk to you tomorrow."

"Yes."

He stood there, his hands fidgeting a bit but his face very still, and looked at me for a moment. Then he looked down and took a small step backward. I didn't know how to react to that, so I just got in the car, closed and locked the door, and started the engine. I gave a little wave goodbye and drove away.

Chapter 15: The Registrar-Recorder/County Clerk

I waited until after rush hour the next morning to drive out to Norwalk, so it only took me about 45 minutes, even with the construction on the freeway. I was glad they were doing that work on the 5. It was pretty bumpy in that area, and full of cracks. I exited at Imperial Highway, which probably was once big enough, compared to other nearby roads, to be considered a highway, but now its three lanes in each direction barely qualify it as a boulevard. It goes from far inland all the way to the ocean, and maybe some parts of it are wider, but calling it a highway now seems like grandiosity.

I passed by what looks like a large park, but which I believe is officially called the Norwalk Civic Center Lawn, and then the Norwalk Regional Library, and then finally turned at the big sign that says "County of Los Angeles Registrar-Recorder/County Clerk". I pulled into the visitor parking lot, which always seems to be full. I had to drive around it twice before a pickup truck with three "Happiness is a Warm Gun" bumper stickers started pulling out of a space in front of me. It wasn't three different bumper stickers. It was three of the same one. One was on the left side of the bumper, one on the right side, and one on the back window. It seemed the owner of the truck really liked warm guns, or at least really liked that bumper sticker. I waited, staying well back, giving it plenty of room. The truck had to back out slowly, because it barely fit in the space, but in my little car I was able to whip right in as soon as the truck was out.

As always, there were people on the steps looking at documents, and others having conversations about documents, or about people who needed to obtain or file documents. I walked up past them and through the glass doors. Inside, there were more people, milling about and talking, or just standing quietly in the various lines. I proceeded past the information desk to the elevators, where more people were waiting, and pressed the down button. When the elevator came I was the only one who got into it. Everyone else was going up. The elevator was noisy but functional, and in a moment the doors opened and I stepped out onto the basement level.

It was much quieter down there, and I didn't see any people. There were piles of boxes in the hallway, as there almost always seem to be. I turned right, maneuvered around some boxes, and headed to room 208.

The door was open. I could see one man behind the counter. His back was to me, but I was fairly sure I recognized the stiff grey hair, the wiry build, and the slightly hunched shoulders.

"Henry?"

He turned to face me.

"Ella! How are you? We haven't seen you here for a while." Henry Park had lived in the United States since he was eight years old, but he still had the ghost of a Korean accent. It wasn't that he mispronounced any words. He actually sometimes enunciated a little too clearly, and there was something else in the rhythms of his speech that felt faintly foreign. Every time I listened to him, I tried to pinpoint exactly what that something else was, but I couldn't quite figure it out.

"And I've missed you guys. Who else is here today?"

"Nadia is digging something out of the files. She'll be back soon."

"Good! How are you? How is your family?"

"Everyone is well. Anne is a junior this year."

"Already?"

"I can't believe it."

"Thinking about college applications?"

"She's already planning her essays. She wants to go to Stanford."

"Good for her. She's certainly capable. Such a smart kid."

"Well, there are many smart kids."

"True, but I'll bet she gets in."

"I hope so. What can we do for you today?"

"I'm looking for a marriage record."

"Just one?"

"I think so."

He pulled out one copy of the appropriate form for me. I wrote in a bride's name of Lucinda Landridge, groom's name unknown.

"How far back does the computer index go? 1985?"

"That's right."

"I'll start there."

I wrote down a year range of 1985-1995. I got out my driver's license and wrote its number on the appropriate line, and signed my name in both necessary places. I handed the form and my license to Henry. He took a quick look at both and handed them back.

"It's all yours." He gestured toward the line of old computers against the wall.

"Thanks, Henry."

He turned back to whatever he had been doing when I arrived, and I walked past shelves of old record books and sat down in front of one of the computers. I had barely gotten started when a woman's voice called my name. I turned and saw Nadia Rodriguez, striking as always, behind the counter. Nadia's mother had idolized Nadia Comaneci, and named her only daughter accordingly, but she made the mistake of having married a very tall man, whose genes Nadia inherited. Nadia never really enjoyed gymnastics anyway, and so was secretly delighted when she turned out to be more suited to basketball. She was the star of her high school team, and her mother became her most devoted cheerleader. Mrs. Rodriguez was again disappointed when her daughter's greatest passion turned out to be filmaking, but then again relieved when Nadia obtained a secure, civil service day job. Mrs. Rodriguez's current concern was a lack of son-in-law or impending grandchildren, but if previous patterns were any guide, she would eventually be granted some form of solace.

Nadia disappeared briefly behind the counter and reappeared through the door with the "employees only" sign on it, taking care not to bang her head on the top of the doorway. I got up to meet her and she bent down to give me a hug. I was struck, both literally and figuratively, by her thick, black, perfectly straight, blindingly glossy hair.

"Nadia, have you grown your hair even longer?"

"I'm thinking of letting it go all the way to my knees."

"It's spectacular, but soon you'll end up stepping on it."

"I thought I might get it to a solid four feet, and then cut it off and give it to one of those charities that makes wigs for cancer patients."

"That's a very generous idea."

"Yeah, I probably won't do it, but I'm thinking about it."

"What are you working on these days?"

"A documentary about Death Valley."

"Really?"

"Yeah. We got some funding from National Geographic. I think this one will be on TV."

"You'll have to tell me when, so I can watch."

"Definitely."

Once I got back to the computer, it didn't take long to find what I was looking for. There are indexes that have been digitized but not put online, and the information I needed was in one of them. In November of 1988, there she was, Lucinda Landridge, age 37, getting married. I was so pleasantly surprised to have found the record that at first her husband's name didn't register. Then it did, and I let out an audible gasp. I looked up. Nadia had gone back to the files, and Henry was engrossed in a pile of papers. I walked back to the counter.

"Henry, may I have a birth record request?"

He handed one to me. I filled out the form, just as I had the marriage record request, writing in my driver's license number and signing in two places. I gave it and my ID to Henry, and he looked at it and gave them back, and I went back to the computer.

Almost immediately, there it was. On the 6th of August, 1991, Lucinda Landridge had a baby boy. I had my answer.

I didn't even bother to go back to the desk and ask for copies of the records. I called out my goodbyes as I gathered my things and rushed out to my car. I got in it and got out my phone, hoping he would pick up right away. He did.

"Roth."

I didn't even say hello. With no preface at all, in a tone of voice bordering on the hysterical, I blurted out, "It's Andrew Cobb!"

"Who?"

"Andrew Cobb. He's a friend of my client, a lawyer. I don't know why he did it, but it had to be him. I just found his birth record. Father Donald Cobb, mother Lucinda Landridge."

"He's Lucinda Landridge's son?"

"Yes."

"And you know this guy?"

"I've met him a couple of times, yes, with my client, the one who led me to Harvey Wilmette."

"Maybe your client is involved too."

"Maybe."

"When were you last in touch with either of them?"

"I saw her on Monday. She asked me to stop by, the day my... oh, wow..."

"The day your house was broken into."

"He wasn't there when I went to see her, but I think he was with her when she called. That little creep broke into my house."

"Maybe."

"I still don't know what he was looking for, though."

"Okay. Slow down. I can't arrest the guy just because of who his mother was."

"Yes, of course. I'm sorry. But it has to be him."

"I can question your client though, about why she asked you to meet her that day, if you are willing to tell me who she is."

"Her name is Sara Markis and she lives in Westwood. I'll text you the address."

"That was quick."

"I'm not a lawyer or a priest. I'm not a private detective or a journalist protecting a source. I'm a genealogist. I won't give you personal information about her or her family without her permission, but there's no reason I can't tell you she's my client. I like to protect my clients' privacy, but if she's connected with a crime, especially one against me, I have no qualms about giving her up."

"All right then. Text me her address."

When I put down the phone, I realized that my heart was pounding. I also knew it would be a long drive home from Norwalk. I took a few deep breaths, started the car, and put on some music. I could think the whole way about why Andrew Cobb would kill Harvey Wilmette, and whether Sara Markis was a willing accomplice or just a naive little nincompoop. I suspected the latter.

Chapter 16: Eavesdropping

I knew I should just go home, but I couldn't stop myself from driving to the police station. I thought I saw that blue sedan I'd thought was following me parked down the street, but it was highly unlikely it was the same car. When I walked in the door I saw Lesley at the front desk. I smiled and calmly asked if it would be possible for me to see Detectives Roth and Vasquez. She picked up the phone and asked, and then led me through the corridor to the big room. Detective Roth saw me as I approached the glass door and waved at an officer near it to let me in.

"Sara Markis is here."

"Now?"

"I shouldn't let you do this, but come on."

He led me to a small office, and warned me to be quiet. We went inside and he carefully closed the door. I could hear voices coming from the next room. He pointed to the two chairs on either side of the desk, which directly underneath an air vent. The carpeting on the floor stopped the chairs from making noise as we pulled them out and sat in them. The voices became more distinct. There were two, Detective Vasquez and Sara Markis.

"Which day last week?"

"I'm pretty sure it was Wednesday. Yeah, Wednesday, I think. Let me just take a look. Um, no, wait, no that's the wrong week. Wait. No. Yeah. Oh, here it is. Right, it was Wednesday. I met my friend there at 7."

"And that was the first time you had ever seen him?"

"Yes, definitely, I mean, as far as I know, that I remember, yeah, that was when I first met him, yes."

"Do you remember what you said to each other? Who spoke first?"

"He did. I was talking to my friend. I was telling her about… It's not like I'm a big gossip or anything, or like I was trying to, like, call attention to myself or something, but, I mean, that kind of thing doesn't happen every day, at least not to me, and it was kind of shocking, you know, and so I wanted to talk about it, with my friend, you know?"

"What exactly were you telling your friend?"

"I was telling her that I hired this genealogist to do research on my grandmother, and the genealogist went to this office, in Hollywood, for information and whatever, and when she got there, there was this dead body, like an actual murdered person. I mean, I know for you that's like, you know, part of your job, but for me it's like, craziness. That kind of thing never happens in my life. At least it never happened before. And now I'm here, in a police station. I have like never in my entire life been in an actual police station. I'm sorry. I'm just, this whole thing just makes me nervous, like really nervous. I'm so sorry, really."

"It's all right. I understand that you're nervous. I'm just trying to find out what happened on Wednesday, what Andrew Cobb said to you."

"Okay. So, I was telling my friend about all that, and he I guess was listening, and he came over to us, and he said something like, 'That must have been so shocking.'"

"That was the first thing he said?"

"Yeah, I think, well, I think first he said, 'I'm sorry to interrupt' or something like that, you know, apologizing for listening in or something, but then yeah, he like, sympathized with how rough it must have been to hear about that, and then he wanted to know about it."

"About what the genealogist told you?"

"Uh huh. He kept asking all these questions, and he was flirting, you know? He was smiling, and looking at me like he liked me, you know? I thought the questions were, like, an excuse to talk to me, but I guess it was the other way around. God! I feel super stupid. So stupid!"

"You're not stupid. It sounds like he was manipulating you."

"Yes! That's exactly, yes."

"So he asked for details about what you'd been told, and you answered his questions."

"Yes."

"And then what?"

"Well, he asked for my number, and I guess I thought he was, I don't know, good-looking or whatever, and I gave it to him."

"And then he called you."

"Yeah, like, a lot. I mean, it seemed like he really liked me. God! So stupid!"

"And he encouraged you to keep meeting with the genealogist."

"Yeah, really encouraged me."

"Okay. Let's move up to Monday. You met with the genealogist again that day, didn't you?"

"Uh huh. He asked me to. He really pushed that. I thought it was kind of weird, but I thought he was just trying to be helpful, because he liked me and all that. God!"

"Was he with you when you called her?"

"Mm hmm, and it seemed like he really wanted to be there when she came over, like, to help me get more information faster or something, and then, when she was on her way, he was like, 'Oh I just remembered I have to be somewhere,' and he just, like, left, and it was so weird, and then she was there and I realized I had like hardly anything to ask her, and I texted him for suggestions, you know, of questions, and he didn't even answer, and it was all so weird and so lame and I felt so stupid, and now I know it's because I WAS so stupid. God!"

"When did you last speak to him?"

"Monday. That was it. He was calling me like, a bunch of times a day for like four days, and then he was all weird that day, and now he like, doesn't even answer texts. So! Stupid!"

"All right. Well, thank you for coming in, Miss Markis. We appreciate your help, and..."

Detective Roth motioned to me to get up, so I did, and we left the room and headed back toward Detective Vasquez's desk.

Finally I could say what I'd been wanting to say since we entered the room: "An air vent? I would have expected a two-way mirror and an intercom."

"We have those, but this wasn't an official interrogation. They were in a conference room."

"Like the one I was in the other day?"

"Exactly like that."

"I won't dwell on the implications of that because I want to know more about what we just heard. She just met him last Wednesday? in some bar?"

"That's what she says, a place called the Cold Mountain Lounge."

"I know where that is, on 21st Street, near my house. I pass by it all the time. It looks like a pretentious hipster outpost. They had a sign out in front recently about being named one of the top ten cool bars in L.A., or something like that."

"Sounds about right."

"Maybe he was following me. Since the day Harvey Wilmette was killed, I've kept feeling like I was being followed. Maybe it was him."

"You didn't tell me you were being followed."

"I thought I was just being paranoid, but maybe I wasn't. If he didn't get what he wanted from Wilmette, and he thought I had information he needed, that would explain the break-in."

"You should have told me."

"So he followed me home, and then, what? He went for a drink nearby, and she just happened to be there? It's quite a coincidence."

"Sometimes they happen," said Detective Roth.

"I suppose."

"We'll check on her story, talk to her friend, and the bartender, and anyone else we can find who was there, but it could be the truth."

"So he kills Wilmette, and then follows me, and then lucks into meeting my client, and pretends to like her so he can find out more about what I'm doing, and then he breaks into my house. But why? What was he looking for?"

"That is the question. Louis Wilmette inherited some money and some paintings and drawings from Rutledge, but the money has long been spent, and all the paintings have been sold. Harvey had tried to sell the few remaining sketches. That was why he met with the art dealer, but what he had left wasn't worth much."

"You've been through everything from Rutledge's will?"

"Everything was meticulously catalogued. Every single work is accounted for. Most are in museums. A few are in private collections, but if he was looking to steal one, he'd have a hard time selling it."

A stray thought entered my mind, an image in my head. It must have showed, because the look on the detective's face grew expectant.

"What if there was another painting, one that wasn't on the list?"

He looked at me more intently.

"What if there was one that wasn't catalogued, because it had never been sold, because it had been given away before he was famous?"

"What?"

"It's a longshot. I mean, it's probably not his. Wouldn't we have known if it was by F. H. Rutledge? And how would Cobb have found out, if we didn't know? But it would make at least some of what's happened make sense."

"What are you talking about?"

I checked the time. It was 8:22. She would be awake. I hoped she was home.

"I need to call my Aunt Louisa."

The detective was starting to look annoyed as well as confused, but he stayed quiet while I called. She answered after just one ring.

"Ella! How are you doing? It's been a while."

"Yes. I'm sorry about that. How are you?"

"Oh, I'm well enough. How are you?"

"I'm fine. I'm sorry. I hate to be rude, but I don't really have time to talk right now. I called because I need to ask you an important question."

"A question about what?"

"About the portrait, the one of your mother."

"Yes?"

"Who painted it?"

"Who painted it?"

"Yes, was it one of her brothers, or was it someone else?"

"You know, I don't know. I suppose I never really thought about it. I always assumed it was one of my uncles. You know they were all painters, all really very good. My mother was quite the artist herself, you know."

"I know. They were a very talented family."

"Yes, they were. I wish I had inherited some of that talent, but I didn't. Not a drop."

"Aunt Louisa, is the painting signed?"

"Oh it must be. Serious painters always sign their work."

"Are you near the dining room? Could you do me a huge favor and take a look?"

"Of course, Ella, if you think it's important. Let me just go see. It might take a minute."

"Take your time. I really appreciate your help."

"What's this all about? Is this something to do with your genealogy projects?"

"Yes, actually."

"Oh! Have you learned something new?"

"I'm not sure, but if that painting is signed, I might have."

"All right. Here it is. It's a bit high up, but if the signature is at the bottom I can probably see it. At least I'm wearing the right glasses!"

There were some rustling sounds.

"Ella, I have to put the phone down for a moment."

"Okay."

There were more sounds of movement, then of the phone being picked up.

"Ella?"

"Yes?"

"It must have been Uncle Fred."

My heart dropped.

"It's signed by Frederick Eylerbetz?"

The detective looked disappointed.

"It looks like it. The signature is hidden by the frame, so I can't see much, but the first letter looks like an 'F'."

I managed not to drop the phone.

"Aunt Louisa, I know it's late and I hate to impose, but would it be all right if I came by and took a look myself?"

Chapter 17: The Kestrels of Pasadena

I had never been so nervous driving anywhere. The detectives had told me to take a direct route and not go too fast, but also to behave normally. I was hoping to be followed, but supposed to be acting as if I had no idea I was being followed. It made a certain logical sense, but I was not used to the layers of subterfuge, and the experience was disconcerting. I felt a little like Dr. Dolittle's pushmepullyou, and it was difficult to concentrate properly. I thought I might have seen the blue sedan, but it was harder to tell the colors of cars in the dark. I took comfort in the knowledge that, even though I couldn't see them, there were police cars somewhere behind me and heading to my destination.

Aunt Louisa's big house in Pasadena looked every bit as imposing at night as it did in the sunlight. The perfectly trimmed lawn and shrubs all had lights perfectly delineating them, as did the house itself. The path and steps from the sidewalk to the front door were also brightly lit. I had no difficulty finding my way.

A maid I hadn't seen before let me in and then left me in the atrium, where an arrangement of yellow roses held the place of prominence on the marble-topped table in the center. I was there only a few seconds before Aunt Louisa came gliding down the wide spiral staircase in pale green chiffon that floated around her as she moved. Enormous jewels on her neck and hands reflected the light in each sconce she passed on her way.

"Ella! It's so lovely to see you. Ana will bring us some tea."

Aunt Louisa had married a wealthy man named Sherman Helford Kestrel, whose family had been in Pasadena for many generations, and she had made the most of her role in society, having no trouble keeping it after he died. When she entertained, even on a small scale, she liked to do it right.

A small table had been set up between two high backed chairs in the corner of the dining room where the portrait of Violet hung. The maid who had let me in, Ana, I assumed, followed us to it pushing a cart designed specifically for the purpose of transporting tea and its accoutrements. She put everything on the table and then took the cart away. The tea was brewed in the proper English way, served with milk, and accompanied by an assortment of tiny cakes and pastries, including real petits fours. I had two. They were worth the drive to Pasadena. Aunt Louisa doesn't mess around.

"I know it's far too late for afternoon tea, but why not?" She swept her arm across the top of the tea and cakes as she said it, like a spokesmodel on a game show. Then she picked up her cup of tea on its saucer, leaned slightly back in her chair, and aimed her eyes at mine like spotlights.

"Don't let me delay you any longer, Ella. You came to look at the portrait. I had the stepladder brought out in case you need it."

Sure enough, there was a stepladder behind her chair, and I did need it. Balanced on the third step, careful to touch the painting as little as possible, I was able to pull the frame away from the canvas just a little and see that after what Aunt Louisa had correctly diagnosed as a capital "F", there was a capital "H". I inhaled sharply.

"Do you see what you were hoping for?"

"I think so."

After the "H" there was a capital "R", and then a lower case "u". It was Rutledge. It was a signed portrait by F. H. Rutledge. I came down from the stepladder and texted the news to Detective Roth.

Aunt Louisa waited for me to walk back around her chair and sit down in mine before she spoke again.

"Now can you tell me what this is all about?"

I told her. We had more tea. She had Ana bring some brandy to put in hers.

"I'm sorry to have to involve you, Aunt Louisa, but I promise every precaution is being taken. We want him to try to steal the painting, but the idea is to catch him before he actually does it. There are police all around, waiting."

"Staking out the place? Like in the movies?"

"More or less."

"Well, Darling Ella, if you think it's a good idea."

"I do."

She sighed gently, and then tossed out a sentence she says nearly every time I see her. "You know your father was the closest thing I had to a son, which makes you the closest thing I have to a granddaughter."

"I know."

She took another sip of tea and leaned toward me, narrowing her eyes conspiratorially. "It's a little exciting, isn't it?"

Aunt Louisa didn't get where she was without her share of guts, and these days not much happened in her life that wasn't expected. As soon as she asked for the brandy, I knew she'd agree to the plan.

When it was all thoroughly explained, I took my leave and headed back to Hollywood. I didn't notice anyone following me, but that didn't mean no one was. Things seemed, as far as I could tell, to be proceeding as they should. Still, I was nervous, and I was glad I was staying someplace with a wall and a gate and a serious alarm system.

There was no news that night or the next morning. At 10:00 a.m. I was glad I had something to do, my final meeting with Sara Markis. I had used up all the hours she had paid for finding a lot of information about the Wilder family, and I was done.

Her street was as peaceful as ever, and her apartment as white. Her fingernails were blue this time, and her feet were in thick socks.

"Hi! Come in! I'm so sorry about your house being broken into. Do they really think Andrew had something to do with it?"

"I don't know. I think they're just questioning everyone I came into contact with. I'm sorry you got dragged into it."

"No, I'm sorry. I mean, if it was connected to that dead body and everything, and you never would have been in that situation if it wasn't for me. I mean, it's so terrible, all these things, you know?"

"I don't know if it was connected though. As far as I know, neither crime has been solved. I assume the police have to examine every possibility. They certainly don't keep me informed about the course of their investigations. I suppose they have to keep that confidential."

"Sure. Yeah, of course. That makes sense."

"So, they questioned your friend Andrew?"

"Well, I guess he's not really much of a friend, and I don't know if they talked to him or not. They talked to me though, like a lot. It was sort of scary, really, and they asked me about him."

"I see."

"They wanted to know when I met him, and when I last saw him, and what we talked about. All kinds of stuff."

"Hmm. What do you mean he's not your friend? I'm sorry if I'm getting too personal, but it seemed like you were close."

"Well, I guess I thought we were getting close, but now I haven't heard from him in a while, kind of a long time, really, so I guess not."

"So, you haven't been in touch with him, since you talked to the police?"

She shook her head. It didn't seem she had any new information or could be any further help in the plan to trap Cobb. I tried to figure out what I could say to change the subject and wrap up the conversation, and finally hit on just the thing. I sighed, shook my head slowly, and said, "Guys."

"I know, right? All super intense for a week and then just nothing."

"Typical."

"Yeah."

She stared at her phone, scrolling halfheartedly.

"So, I think you have everything you need in my report. I still recommend getting a DNA test to be sure, but

I gave you a number of nice looking charts and lots of information that your grandmother might find interesting."

"Oh, yeah, it looks really great. Really, it's so much more than I expected. Thank you so much!"

"You're very welcome. I hope your grandmother likes it."

"Oh she absolutely will. Thank you!"

Yes, it seemed she was just a naive nincompoop. Either that, or a very skilled actress, or possibly both. I felt somewhat less annoyed by her than I had before, though. Perhaps she was growing on me. Maybe it was just that I felt a little sorry for her. In any case, I was glad that project was over.

I enjoyed the stroll back to my car. It was another beautiful day in Southern California. I could hear traffic in the distance, but the birds chirping in the nearby trees were louder. For a moment I almost forgot I was waiting for news about whether or not a trap I'd helped set had succeeded in catching a murderer.

Chapter 18: Getting Some Air

My relative nonchalance did not last long.

It was Friday, so my mother and I had our little shabbat ceremony, and then we had Indian food for dinner. I still hadn't heard anything about Andrew Cobb and Aunt Louisa's painting. I rarely keep my phone on the table during meals, but I did this night. I couldn't avoid being nervous, anxious for updates. My mother was telling me about something. It must have been a description of her day, or some portion of it, but I wasn't actually comprehending any of the words. She must have realized that, because she stopped and looked at me.

"I can see you're preoccupied."

"I'm sorry. I just can't think about anything else."

"Well, that's understandable, in these circumstances. We have plenty of chances to talk. Now we'll just eat."

"Thanks. I really am sorry."

"I know."

She watched me chew a bite of naan.

"They will catch him, Ella."

"Yes, I'm fairly sure they will, but I just can't help feeling anxious."

When dinner was done and cleared I retreated to my room. I put the TV on, but I couldn't even concentrate on that. I managed to pry my phone out of my hands, but I couldn't move it any farther away than on the bed next to me. It was still in my eyeline, and I kept glancing at it.

I had finally just started to doze off when my phone made a sound and I nearly jumped off the bed. It was just a notification that someone I barely remembered had invited me to some sort of event. I stopped reading before I even saw what the event was or when it would take place, and I dropped the phone on the bed. It took me several minutes to get my heart rate back down to a reasonable level.

Eventually, somehow, I fell asleep.

I spent all of Saturday checking my phone. Nothing.

I tried looking up a number of ancestors on my favorite genealogy website, but I didn't find anything useful.

I tried looking up various famous people. Oscar Wilde's family was interesting, but it wasn't enough to distract me from my impatience.

I worked out. Twice. I still couldn't concentrate on anything but waiting for news.

We made salads for dinner. My mother gave up on enticing me into any other topic of conversation and finally just asked me why I thought Andrew Cobb killed Harvey Wilmette.

"I don't think he intended to. I think he went there to find out if Harvey had any useful information, and maybe to give him some kind of manipulative sales pitch."

"Let him in on the deal?"

"Something like that, but then Harvey didn't react the way Cobb wanted him to, maybe even threatened to call the police, and that was it. Rage. Blunt object. Murder."

"What exactly makes you think he'll try to steal the painting from Aunt Louisa? How do you know he knows it's there?"

"I don't even know for sure that he knows it exists, but if he does, if he somehow found out there is an F. H. Rutledge portrait of Violet, and if he found out the Wilmettes didn't have it, didn't even know about it, where would he look next?"

"Violet. And then Violet's family."

"Exactly, and I'm pretty sure he's been following me, and knows I'm here, but this place is extremely hard to get into."

"Luckily for us."

"Yes, and Aunt Agatha lives far away, but Aunt Louisa is not so far, and her house isn't on the top of a mountain and doesn't have walls around it."

"And he very likely followed you there the other day."

"And if you wanted to steal something and you thought it about equally likely to be there or here, wouldn't you try there first?"

"I suppose I would."

"I know it's a lot of ifs, but the police thought the possibility was strong enough to justify watching her house."

"Well, I hope it works."

"The thing I find hardest to understand is, how did he kill Harvey and then just go on looking for the painting, as if nothing had happened? Especially if he didn't intend to do it. Wouldn't that make any decent person feel at least a little guilty, and maybe reconsider the whole endeavor? He seems like a creepy little jerk, but a complete sociopath? It's hard to imagine."

"That's the thing about sociopaths. They don't necessarily make it obvious that they're sociopaths."

"I guess not."

"He probably doesn't think he's a terrible person. He probably thinks Harvey Wilmette's life didn't matter much, at least not as much as whatever it is he wants, money, prestige, revenge, whatever it may be. He also probably thinks it's Harvey's fault he killed him, especially if it was an accident. Harvey made him do it."

"Which are all things only a terrible person would think."

"Yes, but a terrible person wouldn't notice that."

"Right."

I alternated between trying to distract myself with television shows and trying to distract myself by looking things up online. Even my always works, never fails, last resort of dredging Youtube for puppy videos couldn't keep me occupied for long. I looked up wildly random things like the etymology of the word "hazel", which pretty much a dead end, although I did discover that hazel trees symbolize wisdom in both Norse and Celtic mythology. It's

172

amazing what you can learn when you're just trying to waste time.

I decided to take a walk around the grounds before I went to bed. I thought the sound of the gravel pathways under my feet might become hypnotic and help me wind down, but it just sounded loud and irritating, so I left the garden and crossed the lawn toward a stand of trees.

A shadow caught my eye. It wasn't waving in the breeze like the others. I looked at it more directly. It looked like a person, standing near one of the trees. It couldn't be, though. I kept walking, right past the trees and on toward the edge of the property.

I heard something odd, different from the usual night sounds. At first I couldn't place it at all, but then I realized it sounded like breathing, human breathing. I looked again at the shadow by the tree. It was gone.

I glimpsed the dark form next to me just as it lunged toward me. Instinct or reflex pulled me away from a hand as it grabbed at me and caught just the edge of my jacket. I was able to yank it loose and run.

The person was between me and the house, so I ran toward a part of the outer wall where I knew there were trees and bushes big enough to hide behind. At first I could

173

hear breathing close behind me, but then I heard a grunt and a mild thud, followed by some cursing. A root or a rabbit hole must have run interference for me.

I made it to the bushes and hid there. I could see the person running toward me, limping just a little. It looked like a man, in dark pants and a dark sweater. I zipped up my jacket, to make sure the bright yellow lettering on my T-shirt didn't show. I needed to formulate a plan. This hiding place couldn't last long. I focused on examining my options and came up with one that seemed to have potential.

I began working my way along the wall, behind the trees and bushes, farther away from the house and its lights, as quietly as possible. The man continued to run toward the place I had been and then stood there, peering toward the wall. I kept going until I was the shortest distance possible from another, very particular, stand of trees.

The man pulled something out of his pocket. I thought it might be a flashlight. This was the moment to run.

He turned toward me just as I took off. I must have made too much noise pressing through branches. I heard an incredibly loud popping sound, and then another. I made it to the trees. It began to dawn on me that the thing he had pulled out of his pocket was not a flashlight. I took a deep breath, forcing the panic down, and watched him come toward me. If I could get him to the right spot, my plan might still work. I encouraged myself with the thought that he seemed to be a pretty bad shot.

I moved toward the back of the stand of trees, purposely shaking one of the more flexible ones. It worked. He walked in that direction. I stayed very still as he came closer. I could see the gun in his right hand. I tried, not very successfully, to keep my breathing quiet. He couldn't see me, but he knew I was there. I tried to concentrate, to choose my moment carefully.

Some animal made a sudden noise in the distance and the man reflexively turned toward his right. This was it. I crouched down and charged straight at him as fast as I could, aiming for his knees. He went down hard. The wind was knocked out of him, and he dropped the gun. I saw it land a few feet away. I was able to get up and to grab it while he was still trying to breathe. Having never held a gun before, I thought an attempt to use it might not work out in my favor, so I just hung on to it and started running down the hill. Pretty quickly he was able to get up and start running after me.

This part of the property was bounded by fencing, rather than walls, and I headed toward a specific stretch of fence. The slope was getting steeper and I had to be careful not to fall. I could hear his breathing behind me again. I aimed myself very precisely.

I headed right for the fence until I was just a few feet away and then suddenly spun around. Momentum was bringing him right toward me. I ducked down and managed to trip him, making sure to touch him as briefly as possible and get out of the way.

I heard the spark and sizzle as I started running back up the hill toward the house. When it was followed by yelps of pain I knew my plan had worked. The electrified fence wouldn't be enough to knock him out, or even slow him down too much. It was low voltage, only really meant to dissuade animals from entering the property, but at that particular spot, just to the right of where I had stopped, was a patch of cactus covered with very sharp, very painful spines. That would give me a real chance.

He was still not completely deterred, though, and now probably pretty angry. I forced my heart, lungs, and legs to pump as fast as they could. Before long I could hear him behind me, but I was nearly to the house. If I could just open the door I could set off the alarm.

My feet hit the brick of the terrace, and a few seconds later so did his. I just had to get to the door. I heard an odd thunk, and his footsteps stopped. I hit the door, and then looked back as I reached into my pocket for my key. He was lying on the ground, flat on his back, not moving at all. Standing in the dark above him, in her nightgown, was my mother, holding something big and round with a handle.

"Mom? Is that a frying pan?"

"It was the first thing I thought of."

I could hear what sounded like sirens.

"Did you call the police?"

"That should be them."

"The gate?"

"Already opened it."

I opened the door, placed the gun on the floor inside, and closed it again. The sirens had gotten much louder. I walked over to look at the man on the ground. I didn't see any blood, but between the cast iron and the bricks, his head must have been hit pretty hard. I could see his face well enough to be sure that it was Andrew Cobb.

Chapter 19: Ancestors and Descendants

I texted Detective Roth, and he and Detective Vasquez arrived not long after the ambulance, which arrived not long after the first police officers. Cobb regained consciousness, but he had to be taken straight to the hospital.

The police took a lot of photos, and the gun and the frying pan. They let my mother go in and get a robe and slippers, and then Detective Vasquez took her statement. Detective Roth took mine.

"And did he say anything to you?"

"No. He shouted some words, when he tripped and fell over there, and then again after I tripped him, by the fence, but he never talked to me. I wasn't sure it was him until he was unconscious."

"Why did you put the gun on the floor in the hallway?"

"I just wanted to put it in the house. I wasn't sure he wouldn't get up, and I didn't want it to be in easy reach."

"You didn't want to use it?"

"I've never touched a gun before tonight. I thought if I tried to use it I'd probably shoot myself or my mother, or else he would get it from me, and then he would shoot us."

"So you don't know why he was here."

"No, although I guess it must have had something to do with the painting. I really want to know how he got in. It's not easy to get over that wall without alarms going off, and he doesn't strike me as someone with that kind of expertise."

"That's one of the things we'll ask him about."

Something someone said over the police radio caught the detective's attention. He and Detective Vasquez exchanged a look. Then he looked back at me.

"Will you come to the station in the morning?"

"Yes. What's happened?"

"Maybe nothing. We'll finish this tomorrow."

The two detectives rushed off, leaving my mother and me on the terrace, and police officers roaming the grounds with flashlights.

About an hour later, I got a call from Aunt Louisa.

"Ella, I know it's a terrible hour. I hope you weren't asleep."

"I wasn't. Has something happened?"

"I wondered if the police had told you. Apparently not. It seems that man came and tried to take the painting."

"What? That can't be. That man was here, at my mother's house, and he's at the hospital now."

"Well, someone tried to take the painting, and the police took him away. What do you mean he was there?"

"Just what I said. It's all right. No one was hurt except him, and he didn't take anything. Police are here too."

"Goodness! It's a busy night."

"Do you know where they took him? Which police station?"

"I don't know. I assumed the one to which those detectives of yours belong. They're the ones who set the trap, although really the credit has to go to Ana."

"To Ana?"

"Well I suppose the blame also goes to her, because it seems she let him into the house in the first place, but she caught him in the act and got him with Sherman's taser."

"What?"

"Yes! It was still in the center drawer, in that table near the front door. It still worked, after all these years. I didn't even know it was still there, but Ana did, and there you go."

"At some point you will have to tell me all the details, but right now I think I'm going to call those detectives. Do you know what the man's name was, the thief?"

"No, Dear, I didn't catch his name. It was all such a whirlwind."

"Of course. Thanks for letting me know."

"Certainly. Goodnight."

"Goodnight."

I texted Detective Roth and stared at my phone for about a minute. When he didn't answer right away, I got dressed. He still hadn't answered. My mother had gone to sleep, so I left her a note and drove to the police station.

Lesley was at the front desk and let me right in. I was ushered through all the doors and to Detective Roth's desk. After a few minutes, the detective himself appeared.

"I've just seen your text. I'm glad you're here."

"Oh. I was expecting to have to defend myself for coming. I thought you'd be annoyed."

"No. In fact I wanted to ask you about this guy we picked up. His name's Jeremy Blenn. Does that sound familiar?"

"Not at all. That's the guy who tried to take the painting?"

"That's what his ID says. Come look at him. Maybe you've seen him before."

The detective led me down the hall to a small room between two interrogation rooms, each with a big window that I assumed was a mirror on the other side. Andrew Cobb was in one of the rooms, his head bandaged.

"He's had a minor concussion, and he needed a few stitches, but that was it."

"This seems much more professional than the air vent."

He laughed and directed my attention to the other room. The man in it looked young, no more than thirty. He was attractive, fit, with light brown hair and bluish eyes.

"No. I don't know him. Although…"

"Yes?"

"He does look sort of familiar, I think. Maybe. What did you say his name was?"

"Jeremy Blenn. He and Andrew Cobb say they don't know each other."

"Really?"

"Never heard of each other. That's what they both say."

I looked at Cobb in the other room. He looked dejected, pitiful. It was hard to believe that just a few hours before, I was afraid he might kill me. He looked completely harmless now. I thought about when I first saw him, in Sara Markis' apartment. I had disliked him immediately, but I hadn't been afraid of him.

"We are about to put them in a room together, to see how they react. You can stay here and observe, if you'd like."

"I would. Thank you."

The detective left the room for just a moment and then came back. A uniformed police officer entered the room where Jeremy Blenn was sitting and brought him out the door to the hall. Then the door to Andrew Cobb's room opened and the two of them reappeared, along with Detective Vasquez. I didn't notice any spark of recognition between Cobb and Blenn.

"You two seem to be after the same painting. We thought you might want to share strategies, maybe give each other tips."

The two men just stared at each other, both smirking.

"No? Nothing to say to each other? No questions to ask?"

Blenn's smirk expanded into almost a grin."There's nothing this guy can tell me."

"No? What about you, Andrew? Any questions for Jeremy?"

Cobb just kept staring at Blenn, his expression frozen.

"All right then. Party's over."

Everyone but Cobb left the room.

"That's it?"

"For now. Give it a minute."

The uniformed officer soon appeared with Blenn back in the other room. Detective Roth kept watching Cobb.

"Look at him. The wheels are turning in his head."

I turned from looking at Blenn back toward Cobb.

"You're right. It does look like he's thinking pretty hard."

After a moment, we both breathed in sharply, because the look on his face said Andrew Cobb, no genius, had just figured something out. His eyes widened and his cheeks reddened. He swore. He swore again and started pacing around the room. He banged his fist on the table and swore

184

and paced some more. At first his choice of swear words was varied, but soon he settled on repeating one particular word: bitch.

I breathed in sharply again, causing Detective Roth to turn his head to face me. I turned mine to face him.

"I've seen Jeremy Blenn before, not in person, but in a photograph, more than one, actually."

"Where?"

"On a shelf in Sara Markis' apartment."

"That's who he's yelling about?"

"I think so."

Detective Roth left the room and reappeared in the interrogation room with Cobb, who in his fury spilled almost immediately.

"It's her fault I went to that house! It was her plan! She said the painting was there! She drove me there! It was all her! All of it! She even gave me the gun! I think she was trying to get me killed!"

Then he started yelling that same word again.

Sara Markis wasn't in her apartment when the police arrived, but the photos with Jeremy Blenn in them were, and once all the fingerprint results came back everything was clear. His real name was Jerome Markis. He was Sara's cousin, and he had a history of minor thefts and frauds, some of which also involved Sara.

It didn't take long for the Highway Patrol to find Sara's car, and her in it. She was just outside Victorville, on her way to Vegas. It didn't seem like much of an escape plan. If she was the brains of the operation, it was no wonder they all got caught.

All of this took several hours. I refused to go home and sleep, but I wasn't able to stay awake either. I found myself nodding off in what purported to be a chair but seemed more like a prototype for a torture device. When I woke up, without full range of motion in my neck, Sara Markis had arrived and been questioned, and both her apartment and Andrew Cobb's had been thoroughly searched.

Detective Roth was sitting at his desk, not far from me, and noticed my return to consciousness.

"Welcome back."

"I'm not sure I am back."

"I was wondering why you picked that chair."

"I was trying to stay awake."

He laughed and handed me a pair of purple latex gloves.

186

"Here. Put these on."

"Why?"

"Want to see some evidence?"

I put them on.

He handed me an open evidence bag with a book inside. I pulled it out and opened it. It was a diary, with a name written on the inside cover.

"Matilda Landridge! Elbert's sister. Andrew Cobb had this?"

"Yeah. There's a marked page."

He pointed to a spot where an index card had been placed between two pages. I opened it there.

I wish I didn't feel this way. It's jealousy, pure and simple, and it eats at me. I try to be Violet's friend, but it's so hard not to hate her. I know she's beautiful, and talented, but everyone loves her. Why him too?

I went to the studio today to bring Elbert some sandwiches. He was working on a charming picture of ships on the lake. I was very happy to see that Frank was there too, but then I saw what he was working on. It was a portrait of her. I didn't know she had sat for him. He was

putting finishing touches on her hair, and then her hands. I
very nearly started to cry.

"Poor Matilda. How sad."

"I think you're missing the point."

"No, I get it. That's how Cobb knew the painting existed, or at least had existed at some point. Still, I feel sad for her."

"Leaving aside feelings, it's evidence. There's more about the painting in the diary. We also found a copy of Rutledge's will, with the full catalogue of works, and that painting is not on the list."

"He must have given it to Violet, soon after he painted it. I didn't know he was in love with her, although I guess we have only Matilda's word for that. Maybe he just wanted to paint her."

"Maybe. There's something else you should see too."

He handed me another evidence bag. This one contained a genealogical chart of Violet Eylerbetz Graepenteck and all her descendants, including me. Of course Aunt Louisa and her husband Sherman Kestrel were on it too.

"So, Andrew Cobb reads this diary and suspects this painting still exists, a genuine F. H. Rutledge painting that no one knows about, that isn't in any catalogue, and he goes to the Wilmette heirs to find out if they know about it."

"Exactly."

"And when he gets nothing from Harvey he figures Violet's family might know something, or even have the painting."

"Right."

"Has he admitted that?"

"Not yet. We're just about to put a little pressure on. Want to see?"

I nodded.

"Come on."

Chapter 20: Murderers and Thieves

We went back to the observation room between the two interrogation rooms. Cobb was by himself in one. Sara and her cousin were together in the other, along with Detective Vasquez. Sara was crying. Her cousin was leaning back in his chair, as far as he could go with his handcuffs through a metal loop on the table, looking smug. The detective was talking.

"The thing is, Jerome, you forgot to make sure there were no fingerprints on the bullets. If there's no connection between you, how did Cobb get a gun that had bullets in it with your fingerprints on them?"

Jerome shrugged.

"I think it's pretty obvious. Sara, you got the gun from Jerome, and you gave it to Cobb."

She shook her head vigorously.

"No, Detective, you don't understand. I didn't give it to him. He took it. He just, like, took it."

"Why did you have it in the first place? Why did you ask Jerome to get it for you?"

"I was scared! I was so, so scared! I just, I didn't know what to do!"

At that, she erupted in loud sobs.

In the other interrogation room, a uniformed officer came in, checked Andrew Cobb's handcuffs, and then led him out into the hall. A few seconds later, the door opened in the first room, and Detective Vasquez, Jerome, and sobbing Sara looked up to see Cobb walk in.

He immediately lunged for Sara, which shocked her out of her sobs, but the officer had a good hold on him, and Detective Vasquez jumped up in front of him, so all he managed to do was lean toward her a bit.

The police officers managed to calm him down and get him seated across the table from Jerome, his handcuffs attached to the table the same way Jerome's and Sara's were. The officer who had come in with Cobb stood against the wall at the end of the table near him. Another officer came in and stood by the door.

I could see Sara's and Jerome's faces. I couldn't see Andrew's, but I could see the tension in his back. Detective Vasquez sat down next to him, across from Sara.

"So, Andrew, why are you so angry at Sara?"

He didn't answer, but Sara looked nervous.

"She was just telling me how you stole that gun from her, the one she got from her cousin here for her protection, because she was so darn scared. Isn't that right, Sara? You said he took it from you?"

Cobb tried to stand up, but the officer near him pushed him back down. He opted for yelling at Sara instead.

"Liar! You can't put all this on me! You and your creepy cousin! You think I can't figure it out? Pretending to be all innocent and making me a decoy? I could have been killed!"

Sara stared at her own hands, looking more and more worried. Jerome was much calmer. He laughed. That drew Andrew's attention.

"Oh yeah? You think you're so cool? You're here in handcuffs too!"

"At least I'm not a murderer."

"I'm not a murderer! Did she say I'm a murderer? I didn't murder anybody!"

Jerome laughed again. Cobb turned toward Detective Vasquez.

"I didn't go there to kill the guy! She's lying if she said that! I just wanted to know about the painting! He just got so freaked out! He was going for the phone! What was I supposed to do? I didn't think he was going to die! I just hit the guy one time! Just one time!"

Jerome's smirk was taking over his whole face.

"You're right, Sara. He's an idiot."

Andrew tried to lunge for Jerome, but his handcuffs and the officer stopped him. Detective Vasquez had a new question.

"Jerome, why don't you tell Andrew about how you got caught?"

Jerome's smirk shrank a little.

"Why don't you tell him how you got tased by the maid, how she had you all wrapped up in extension cords when the police arrived?"

Andrew settled back in his chair, relaxed a bit, and laughed.

"Yeah, Jerome, why don't you tell me about that?"

"Have you ever been tased? It's no joke!"

Andrew laughed again. "The maid caught you? All by herself?"

"Shut up."

"Just her and her taser. How did you get in, anyway? Break a window?"

"Charm, dude, charm. You wouldn't know anything about that."

"What? So she let you in and then she tased you?"

"No, idiot, she let me in the day before. I saw her alarm code. Who's awake and wandering around a big house like that in the middle of the night anyway? Just bad timing, man, not my fault."

"And you call me an idiot?"

"Yeah, dude, you just admitted to murder."

"It was an accident!"

Sara looked very happy to let the two of them keep yelling at each other, but Detective Vasquez interrupted.

"So, Andrew, didn't you say Sara drove you over to Patricia Graepenteck's house?"

Andrew stopped yelling at Jerome.

"Didn't you say she dropped you off there in the afternoon and told you how to get past the gate?"

"Yeah. It was all her idea. I didn't need a code or anything. I just hid in the bushes outside the wall until someone drove in, and then I ran in behind the car and hid in the bushes inside the wall until it got dark."

194

Sara cranked up the tears again.

"Andrew, why are you saying these things? You're like, literally just making up total lies!"

Before he could start yelling again, Vasquez asked Sara another question.

"You didn't drive him to the house?"

"Of course not. Why would I do that?"

"That's interesting, because we found plant matter and soil on your car that looks like an exact match to the area right by that house."

"But that stuff must be the same, like, all over L.A."

"No, it's actually not. There are some fairly rare plants that grow in that particular spot."

"Well, um, I don't know how it got there."

"Did someone else drive your car?"

Sara looked at Jerome, but he wouldn't bite. He just shook his head.

Andrew started laughing again. "You're stuck now, Babe! They got you!"

Sara hadn't given up yet. Somehow she manufactured still more tears.

"It was Andrew. It was totally him. He made me do it. I didn't want to, but I found out about, you know, how he killed that guy…"

"It was an accident!"

"I knew he like actually killed that guy, and I was just so, so scared, and he took that gun, and he made me go there, and…"

Detective Vasquez stood up.

"Wait, Detective, you have to believe me! It wasn't my fault!"

The detective motioned to the uniformed officers, and they unhooked Andrew Cobb from the table, and the three of them followed him out of the room.

As soon as they were gone, Sara's tears miraculously stopped flowing. Her cousin's smirk was as big as ever.

"I told you it wouldn't work."

"Shut up, Jerome!"

After that they just sat there glaring at each other.

I was startled by a loud noise behind me. Detective Roth and I both turned toward it at the same time. A woman was in the other interrogation room, pounding on the mirror/window.

"I know someone's in there!" she yelled, and then pounded again. "Let me see my son!"

Her age was unclear, because her face had the inhuman look of extensive plastic surgery, and it was covered in a thick layer of makeup. Her hair was the color of the inside of a lemon, and it displayed the volume and discipline only the recent touch of a professional hairdresser could have provided. She was wearing something that was probably a knock-off but looked like a Chanel suit.

She cupped her hands around her eyes, trying to see through the window. Her fingers and wrists boasted heavy rings and bracelets. I wondered if they could scratch the coating on the glass. She didn't seem to have thought of that, but she hit the window one more time. "My lawyer is on his way!"

"That must be Lucinda Landridge Cobb."

"Yes."

"How long has she been in there?"

"A few minutes."

"Will she get to see Andrew?"

"Any moment now."

She turned away from the window and walked over to the table and sat down, her legs carefully crossed. Her shoes were very shiny. The heels had to be at least six inches high, and they tapered down to tiny points. She must have had a lot of practice walking on those things. I'd bet she could run in them. I'd break my ankle if I tried, not that I'd ever bother trying, but I had to admire her skill.

The door to the hall opened and a uniformed officer asked her to come with him. She stood up gracefully, announced, "It's about time!" and, without a trace of wobble on those precarious shoes, followed him into the hall.

Two more officers arrived to take Sara and Jerome away, and I went with Detective Roth back to his desk. He offered me a relatively comfortable chair and a cup of tea.

"I have paperwork to do on all this. It's probably boring, but if you're curious, you could stick around and see how it's done, at least until you finish your tea."

"I'm always curious."

Not much later, there was movement from down the hall. Two uniformed officers were walking toward us, with a handcuffed Andrew Cobb between them. His head was high, his nose and chin pointed toward the ceiling. His mother was walking behind him. When he saw me, he turned his head and said something to her that caused her to glare at me. They both stared at me as they came closer, their eyes overflowing with the kind of emotion you'd expect to see during a contentious divorce proceeding. I thought one or both of them might actually spit at me, or at least yell at me, but they didn't. They just tossed their heads as they passed, his natural brown hair and her expensive blond hair whipping to one side and then settling back into their carefully coiffed styles.

I sipped my tea as I watched them go through the glass door, and then through the door to the main hallway. Then I turned back to Detective Roth.

"Does that mean he's getting bail?"

"Most likely."

"He's going to jail though, right?"

"Oh yeah."

"I can't believe he confessed so completely."

"It happens more than you'd think. He felt justified in what he did. He was only trying to get what he thought he deserved."

"Hardly anyone ever gets what that man thinks he deserves."

199

Detective Roth looked at me and smiled. If I hadn't been so exhausted, I think I might have blushed.

Chapter 21: Mysteries

Eventually I decided I ought to go home. Detective Roth offered to walk me out to my car.

He held the glass door for me, and then the door into the hallway, where Lesley happened to be stationed. I smiled at her as we passed by, and she smiled back.

The detective and I walked silently down the hall and entered the main lobby. The dark haired young woman who had been at the front desk the first time I came to the station was there again. She was on the phone and barely acknowledged us as we walked past.

We emerged from the fluorescent light and air-conditioning into the shaded walkway from the front door to the sidewalk, and then gradually toward the sunlight and its attendant heat. I just kept walking toward my car, and he just kept walking with me. It was as quiet out there as it ever gets in Hollywood, which is to say I heard no sirens or loud music, and the traffic noise was mostly distant. I thought I heard a bird singing, but it might have been someone's ringtone. It seemed like the relative silence had lasted long enough, so I broke it.

"I guess I'm not in any danger anymore, from break-ins, or anything like that."

"No, not now that everyone knows where the painting is."

"And it doesn't look like there will be any dispute about the ownership of the painting."

"No. It was never catalogued or mentioned in Rutledge's will or any documented letters, and the only people who seem ever to have owned it were your great grandmother, who was the subject of it, and your great aunt, so it's hard to come up with any plausible argument that it wasn't given as a gift. I think it pretty safely belongs to your Aunt Louisa."

"And now it has more than just sentimental value."

"A lot more."

We stopped walking because we had reached my car. I noted that its cheerful blue color was almost exactly the same as the sky at that moment, but that thought didn't relax me at all. I felt surprisingly nervous, and hyper-aware of the proximity of Detective Roth. He was standing right next to me. The distance between my arm and his was no more than a few inches. It seemed like I should turn to look at him and say thank you and goodbye, but I found it, somehow, physically difficult to do that. I couldn't seem to turn my head, so I just stood there and stared at my car. I began to feel more and more like an idiot.

I felt, rather than saw, that he made some kind of movement, fidgeting with his hands, perhaps. Finally he said something.

"Ms. Graepenteck."

Something about the way he said it turned my face toward him, without my intending it, like a reflex. He kept talking.

"I want to say thank you, for your help in this investigation."

"Thank you, for letting me help. It was such an interesting experience, aside from the fact that I was a suspect. That part was not much fun, but the rest, the process. I learned a lot."

"Sorry about that, the suspect part."

"No need to apologize. It made sense. I would have suspected me too. There were all those crazy coincidences." I was just making conversation, but he seized on that word.

"But they weren't really coincidences at all, not most of them, anyway, not if you look at it from the perpetrator's perspective. He went after Wilmette because he was Rutledge's heir, and you showed up at Wilmette's office. You're a genealogist, so you could have been tracing heirs, so you'd be a good lead for him. Sara Markis was your client, so she could have been the heir. Then when he found out you were descended from the subject of the painting, it would have seemed obvious that you'd be his best route to find it. The only real coincidence was that you, the descendant of Violet Eylerbetz, ended up in the office of the heir of F. H. Rutledge, and even that was not so strange, given that he traded in memorabilia that included Violet's nephew."

"You're right. When you explain it that way, it doesn't sound so odd. I guess that's what you have to do, in your work, look at it from the perpetrator's perspective."

"It helps."

"I'm glad I don't have to do that. I do occasionally come across criminals in my work, but not very often, and when I do, they are usually long dead, and their crimes are very old."

"Not this time."

"No, but I hope this is the only time there's an actual live criminal and a current crime. I at least hope there's never another crime against me."

"I hope that too, that last part, anyway."

The green parts of his eyes seemed especially bright. It must have been the way the sunlight was hitting them.

I unlocked my car and opened the door. As I got into the front seat, he said, "Drive safely." His use of the grammatically correct adverb made me want to jump up and kiss him, but I didn't. I just said, "Thanks. Bye!" and closed and locked the car door. As I pulled away, we waved and smiled at each other, and then I headed for the freeway.

The next day I was surprised to get a call from Bob Ogilvie.

"The police called and told me they caught Harvey's murderer, and you helped them do it, and, well, I just wanted to thank you. I'm not sure I understand why the fellow did it, something to do with a painting?"

"Yes, by F. H. Rutledge."

"Oh, right, yes, I've heard of him."

"I'm glad they solved it, pretty quickly too."

"Yeah, they did a good job. Doesn't change anything for Harvey though."

"I suppose not."

"Still, it's nice to have it wrapped up."

"Are things getting at all back to normal for you?"

"Oh, I don't know about normal, but, well, life goes on."

"Yes. What about Harvey's brother and his wife?"

"Oh, I guess James and Miranda are all right. Nothing much has changed for them."

"No?"

"Nah, not really. You know, I don't mind telling you, after all, you were there when we all found out, about the insurance money…"

"Right."

"Well, Barbara has been very generous. She's paying off all Harvey's debts, and the company's debts."

"That is generous."

"She's a kind woman, Barbara."

"It seems so."

"Yeah, so, I'm selling off the inventory, as much as I can, and then I think I'll just close down the business and retire."

"Really?"

"Yeah, it's time, and it's not the same without Harvey, you know?"

"Sure. I guess that makes sense."

"Yeah."

"While you're clearing out the inventory, I wouldn't mind having whatever you've got on Reginald Ellis. How much would that cost?"

"Oh, I won't charge you. Give me an address and I'll have it sent over."

"That's very generous of you."

"Oh, well, I guess it's contagious."

I'd cleaned up my bedroom and office, and not found anything missing. Everything seemed pretty much back to normal.

I thought about Andrew Cobb, and Lucinda Landridge, and her father and grandfather. It must have been difficult for Elbert Landridge to see all his friends and colleagues doing so well, while his and his family's fortunes just kept declining. I wondered if he had asked for help, or if he had been too proud. You can't get those kinds of details from census records and death certificates. Those are the blank spaces documentation doesn't fill.

A siren blared in the distance. I wasn't sure if it was police or a fire truck or an ambulance. I think there are differences in the specific sounds, but I can never keep them straight. One of the neighborhood dogs was barking.

Poor Harvey Wilmette. I was glad his killer would go to jail, but it didn't seem like enough. I didn't know what kind of life he'd had, if he'd been happy or not, but it seemed wrong that Andrew Cobb was able so easily to take whatever he did have away from him.

A couple of months later, when the ordeal was finally losing its priority placement in my thoughts, my phone rang. It was Detective Roth.

"Ms. Graepenteck, Detective Vasquez and I have caught an unusual case, and there may be a genealogy angle. We were wondering if you would be interested in doing some consulting work, and helping us out."

I'd like to say I hesitated a moment, that I thought about how difficult those two weeks had been, not just for me, but also for my family, that I considered the potential dangers and weighed them against the possible good I could do by helping to solve a crime, but I didn't do any of that. I didn't even ask for any details about the case. I just said, right away, with no thought at all, "Yes, Detective Roth. Yes, I would."

Thank you for reading *The Moving Pictures*! If you enjoyed it, or even if you didn't, please post a review wherever you read reviews, and share your opinion with the world.

Someone at this very moment is trying to decide whether or not to buy this book, and a review from you could help that person immensely.

Please visit esteigerandco.com if you would like to know more about author Erika Maren Steiger and her other books.

Appendix: Family Trees

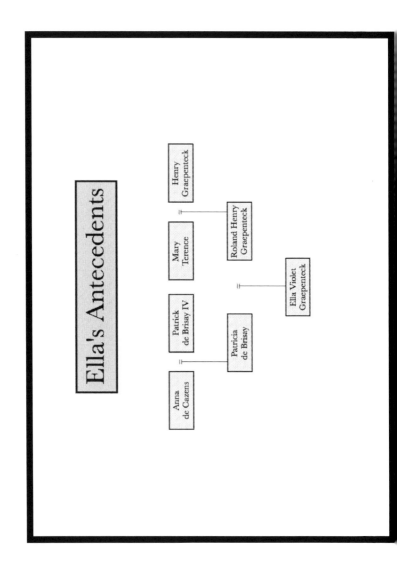

Ella's Antecedents

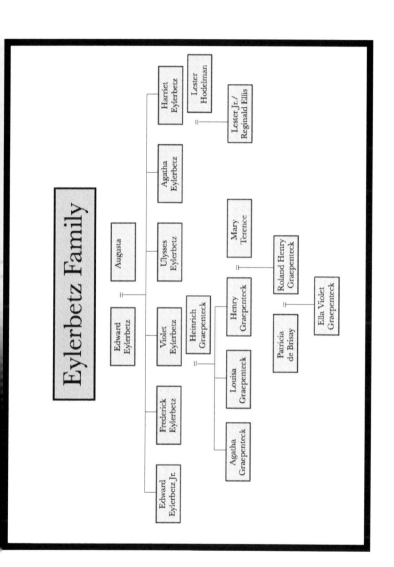

Eylerbetz Family

Edward Eylerbetz = Augusta

Edward Eylerbetz Jr. — Frederick Eylerbetz — Violet Eylerbetz — Ulysses Eylerbetz — Agatha Eylerbetz — Harriet Eylerbetz

Violet Eylerbetz = Heinrich Graepenteck

Agatha Graepenteck — Louisa Graepenteck — Henry Graepenteck — Mary Terence

Harriet Eylerbetz = Lester Hoderman

Lester Jr./ Reginald Ellis

Henry Graepenteck = Mary Terence

Louisa Graepenteck = Roland Henry Graepenteck

Patricia de Brisay = Ella Violet Graepenteck

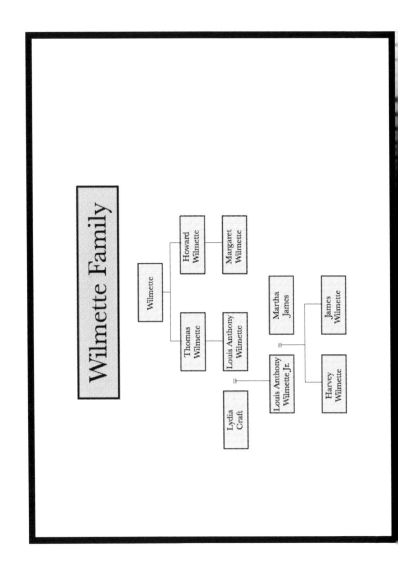

Wilmette Family

- Wilmette
  - Thomas Wilmette
    - Louis Anthony Wilmette
      - Louis Anthony Wilmette Jr. = Lydia Craft
        - Martha James =
          - Harvey Wilmette
          - James Wilmette
  - Howard Wilmette
    - Margaret Wilmette

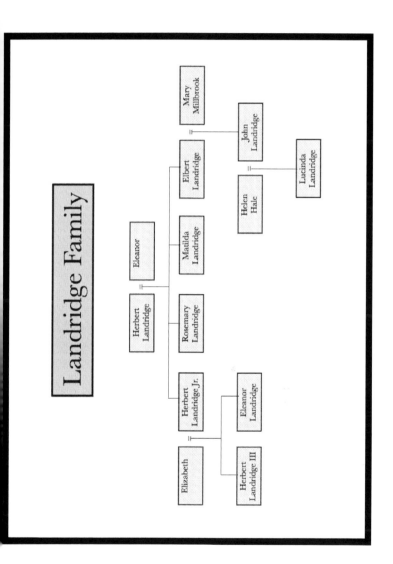

Landridge Family

Acknowledgements

There are hundreds of people I ought to thank, for inspiration, encouragement, and advice, but I will restrict it to three. The first is the marvelous playwright, indispensable critic, and wonderful friend Kimberly Kalaja, without whom I would probably never have finished. The second is my father, Paul E. Steiger, whose encouragement and specific suggestions were invaluable. The third is my mother, JoAnn McKenna, whose support and unfailing belief in me extend far beyond the limits of good sense, and without whom I would never have had the courage to start.

Printed in Great Britain
by Amazon